Ruth Prawer Jhabvala

The Householder

Penguin Books

Penguin Books Ltd, Harmondsworth,
Middlesex, England
Penguin Books, 625 Madison Avenue,
New York, New York 10022, U.S.A.
Penguin Books Australia Ltd, Ringwood,
Victoria, Australia
Penguin Books Canada Ltd, 2801 John Street,
Markham, Ontario, Canada L3R 1B4
Penguin Books (N.Z.) Ltd, 182–190 Wairau Road,
Auckland 10, New Zealand

First published by John Murray 1960
Published in Penguin Books 1980

Set, printed and bound in Great Britain by
Cox & Wyman Ltd, Reading
Set in Intertype Times

Penguin Books
The Householder

£1-95

Ruth Prawer Jhabvala was born in Germany of Polish
parents and came to England at the age of twelve. She was
educated at Queen Mary College, London University, and
began writing after graduation and marriage. Her
published work includes four collections of short stories,
*Like Birds, Like Fishes, How I Became a Holy Mother,
A Stronger Climate* and *An Experience of India*; and the
novels *To Whom She Will, The Nature of Passion, Esmond
in India, Get Ready for Battle, A Backward Place, A New
Dominion* and *Heat and Dust*, winner of the 1975 Booker
Prize.

She has also collaborated on several film scripts, among
them *Shakespeare Wallah* and *Autobiography of a Princess*,
and has written a number of plays for television. Ruth
Jhabvala won the Neil Gunn International Fellowship
in 1978

For Renana, Ava and Firoza-Bibi

1

Prem sat at the only table they had and corrected his students' essay papers. The table was a very frail and shaky one, made of thin cane, and it would have been more comfortable to sit on the floor. But he felt there was a certain dignity about sitting at a table; his father had always sat at a table when correcting papers. It was unreasonable, of course, to consider dignity, when there was no chance of any of his students seeing him; but he considered he would feel better for it afterwards, when he was returning their papers. He was not too good at enforcing discipline, and that made him a little afraid of his students and in need of all the moral support he could give himself.

It was a Sunday evening, and correcting papers, he felt, was not a very good way of spending it. But he had as yet no friends in Delhi and knew of no places to go to. He had been for a walk earlier in the evening, but walking by oneself was depressing. He had sauntered down the road, past the compound where the milkman's four black buffaloes lived and past the sewage canal and the municipal Family Planning clinic. It had been very boring. Afterwards he had gone and sat for a few minutes in the children's park, watching the children go round and round on the stiff little wooden seats of the roundabout; and on the way home through the street of the bazaar, he had jingled the coins in his pocket and wondered whether to buy himself a bag of nuts and raisins or not. Sometimes he thought yes and sometimes he thought no; not because of the money, but because of Indu. He considered that if he bought a bag for himself, he would have to bring one for her too. But he felt shy of doing so. He had never yet brought her a gift, and he did not know in what way to offer it to her; nor did he know how she would accept it from him. In the end he bought just one bag of nuts and raisins and ate it by himself, throwing away the paper before he reached home. But he ate it so quickly and guiltily that he did not enjoy it at all.

'Afterwards,' he read, 'there was a great crush of people and many children cried and also were lost to their parents.' He had given his students an essay to write on the Republic Day Parade. None of them had anything interesting to say on the Parade itself, but they all expressed moral sentiments of a high order. 'How beautiful to see our Country, our Bharat, so feasted and loved,' they wrote; or 'Thus was offering of thanks given to God and our good and great Prime Minister for our Freedom and Independence.' When Prem came across a particularly good sentiment like that, he ticked it and wrote 'Very good', even if there was a mistake in spelling or grammar. He was often surprised, when correcting papers, at the deep thoughts and feelings his students expressed. In the classroom they seemed such callow young men, one would never have credited them with any of these finer sentiments.

Indu yawned, rather loudly, which irritated Prem. Why should she be tired? She had done no work. She was sitting on the floor, stitching a blouse for herself. Once or twice he had heard her very quietly sigh. That too had irritated him, for he did not see that she had any cause for unhappiness, for the burden of providing for her and for himself, for paying their rent and their food and their servant-boy, was all his. And now she was pregnant. He had already had to pay five rupees to a doctor for confirming that fact. Her pregnancy was a terrible embarrassment for him. Now everybody would know what he did with her at night in the dark, as quickly and guiltily as he had eaten the nuts and raisins. And besides the embarrassment, there was the worry. Soon he would have a family and his expenses would mount; but his salary at Mr Khanna's college was only 175 rupees a month. How to manage on that? His rent alone came to 45 rupees.

What he needed was a better-paid job. He had been thinking of it for some time now, ever since he had learnt that Indu was pregnant, but this evening it occurred to him for the first time to glance through old newspapers and see what kinds of likely jobs were being advertised nowadays. He got up to go into the kitchen where he knew Indu stored the old newspapers. She used some for lighting the fire and collected the rest in order to sell them to the rag, bottle and paper man who paid a good price for them.

While he was crossing the landing to go from their sitting-room to their kitchen, he heard the noise from the Seigals downstairs. The Seigels were their landlords and occupied the downstairs portion of the house. They were very jolly people, and every evening they had visitors. Mr Seigal played cards with the men – they all sat round a little card-table under a lamp, drank whisky and slammed down their cards with gusto; sometimes they laughed and made jokes, sometimes they shouted and quarrelled. The ladies sat on the veranda and knitted and talked. The Seigals' son Romesh twiddled with the radio and when he got some good film music, he loudly joined in; he knew all the film songs, for he went to the cinema three times a week. Prem stood on the landing and listened to him. He could also hear Mr Seigal laughing and thumping the table over some very good story. Tea-cups rattled on a tray and all the lights were blazing.

Prem's kitchen was bare and empty. The servant-boy was, as usual, out (he had many friends in the district). Prem found the newspapers piled up by the fire-grate and sat down on the floor to look through them. Some had already been torn for lighting the fire and had the advertisement pages missing. But even in those in which he still found the advertisements, there were no jobs for him. Only for engineers and draughtsmen and doctors. Nobody seemed to want a Hindi teacher; or if they did, they wanted him to be a first-class M.A. with three years' teaching experience, not a second-class B.A. with only four months' teaching experience, such as he was. He sat on the floor in the kitchen, with the newpapers spread round him, and felt a terrible oppression. He was so young; only a very short while ago he had been a student and he had lived at home with his parents who had looked after him and he had had no responsibility except to pass his examinations. His mother had gone round the house with her finger on her lips and she said to everyone who came, 'Sh, Prem is studying for his examinations.' And she had cooked big meals for him to build up his strength. Not like the tasteless food Indu served to him. He realized that he felt a great dislike for Indu. Why had they married him to her? She was not even very pretty.

Because there were no other jobs for him, he realized he would have to improve on what he had. He would have to ask the Principal of his college for a rise in salary. It was not something he liked to do, but that only increased his conviction that he must do it. When his father was still alive, he had always told him 'Put all your strength into doing the things you don't like to do', and Prem had taken the lesson to heart. So all the way to the college he was saying to himself, 'I don't like to do it, therefore I must do it.' He was frowning with concentration, keeping himself up to this resolution, which had one good result, for in his preoccupation he hardly noticed that he had reached the college. Usually he felt great embarrassment on reaching the college, for many students stood lounging outside, leaning against the wall with their hands in their pockets and looking with bored and critical eyes at all passers-by. Prem hated having to pass and be inspected by them, it made him feel more inadequate.

It was a pity the students had nowhere to go before and after classes except out in the street; but the college was only an ordinary residential house in the middle of a street consisting of other ordinary residential houses, so there was no question of grounds. Between classes the students had either the corridor or the street, and most of them preferred the street. Consequently the college had a bad name in the neighbourhood and letters of complaint were constantly being sent to the Principal ('Sir, I wish to bring to your notice that my daughter cannot pass your college without being affronted by your students with remarks that are not proper for a young unmarried girl to hear.') At regular intervals the Principal would call the whole college together in the biggest class-room, which had to serve as assembly-hall on such occasions, and he would tell the students how the college had always had a good name and that this good name must be preserved at all costs, and that, therefore, he would expel – 'without mercy', he said, looking sternly round the room – any student who did not know how to behave himself. But though he spoke very severely, occasionally pounding his fist on a desk, he never did expel anyone because he could not bear to refund the fees.

All the rooms were divided in the middle to accommodate two classes each. The students of the two different classes sat with their backs to one another, but the teachers faced each other from their dais and blackboards at opposite ends of the room. Prem, who was in charge of the Hindi class, shared a room with Mr Chaddha, the professor of history. Mr Chaddha was a birdlike little man who managed to keep discipline very well, so that his end of the room was always very much quieter than Prem's. All his students were already seated on their benches, arranging their notes, while only two or three of Prem's students had arrived and casually lounged around leaning over to talk to one another. One of them was even smoking. Irritated by this contrast between his own and Mr Chaddha's students, Prem said, more sternly than he would otherwise perhaps have done, 'Smoking in the classroom is not allowed.' 'I am just finishing this one, sir,' said the student, quite easy and friendly; so now Prem did not know whether to force the issue or let it pass. (This was a dilemma he faced several times a day, for he feared on the one hand to be too strict with the

10

students, on the other to lose their respect.) Finally he let it pass. Since he had definitely decided to ask Mr Khanna for a rise in salary that very morning, he had, he considered, a hard enough task before him and did not wish to exhaust his mental energy beforehand.

At nine-thirty there was a break, so he went to the staffroom to drink the cup of tea which was supplied from Mrs Khanna's kitchen and for which each member of staff paid two rupees eight annas a month. The staffroom was not always a staffroom, for when Mr Khanna had guests, he used it as a guest-room, bringing in a bed and a towel with 'Work is Worship' embroidered on it. While the guests remained, the professors had to drink their tea either in the corridor or in their own classrooms. This was most awkward for Mr Sohan Lal, the professor of mathematics, who lived in Mehrauli and had to leave his home at six o'clock in the morning to come cycling to the college. He always brought his breakfast with him in a tin tiffin-carrier, as well as a thermos flask of tea since he could not afford to pay Mrs Khanna's two rupees eight annas. He felt very shy while eating his food and sat in a corner with his head turned delicately away while he chewed. When the staffroom was not available, he would often go without his food because he could not find a quiet retreat in which to eat it.

Prem knew how shy Sohan Lal felt while eating, so he did not go to sit near him, though he enjoyed his company more than that of any of the other professors. Instead he sat by Mr Chaddha, whose company he did not enjoy at all. Indeed, Mr Chaddha took no notice of him, but sat there in an armchair in the middle of the room with his legs crossed, swinging one little foot and reading a book; when he came to an interesting point in his reading, he exclaimed 'Ha!' and made a bold pencil-mark in the margin.

The Principal's private residence took up the first floor of the house. Prem stood hesitating outside the sitting-room door, but he made himself be brave and entered. Mr Khanna was sitting eating his breakfast. 'Yes, come in!' he called. 'Don't be shy!' But Prem was shy; he hovered by the door and kept his eyes lowered. Mr Khanna was in a jovial mood. 'You see me enjoying my breakfast,' he explained. Prem looked up and nodded. He saw that Mr Khanna was having an English breakfast of eggs and toast.

'It is very important to start the day with a good breakfast,' Mr Khanna said. Prem nodded again. He could not speak, he was so overwhelmed with shyness. Not only because of what he had come to

11

say, but also because the Principal's sitting-room always made him feel shy. Everything was new and opulent and comfortable – plump cushions and flowered curtains and a big shiny radio-set; and Mr Khanna himself so cheerful and self-confident, wearing a nicely laundered shirt and mopping up his egg with a piece of toast.

'You see,' explained Mr Khanna, 'the gastric juices must be allowed to flow from early morning, otherwise they will become clogged and nasty indigestions follow.'

Quite unreasonably, Prem thought of Sohan Lal eating his first humble meal perched on a little bench in the staffroom. And this thought made him say quite the wrong thing: 'Please sir,' he said, 'Mr Sohan Lal lives in Mehrauli.'

'I know it,' said the Principal. He finished chewing a bite of toast and added 'It is a long way'; there was even a note of sympathy in his voice which encouraged Prem to think he had started on a good line.

'A very long way, sir,' he said. He took a step forward and earnestly looked at the Principal. 'He has to leave his house at six o'clock in the morning, without any food.'

Mr Khanna nodded, again with sympathy. He shook some salt from a container and said, 'You should always take plenty of salt with your food. It quickens the energies.'

'Sir,' said Prem, 'Mr Sohan Lal has a large family to support.'

'A spoonful of salt taken in a glass of warm water is also very good for replacing liquid strength lost through too much perspiration. You see, in our climate we must take great care of the body.'

'He has not only his mother, his wife and his own children, but also his brother's family to take care of. His brother died four years ago of fever.'

'In our climate there are many different kinds of fever we have to guard against.'

'It is very difficult for him to manage on his present salary, 'Prem said. 'How can he support so many people on 175 rupees a month?' He took another step forward and said in a voice passionate with conviction and pity, 'Poverty and want are terrible things. In the Panchatantra it is written "It is better to be dead than poor".'

Mr Khanna said, 'It is an interesting thought.'

'It is also a very sad thought, sir,' Prem said.

'Ah yes,' said Mr Khanna with a sigh. He left a moment's respectful silence, then said in a matter-of-fact business tone, 'He has sent you to ask for a rise in salary?'

'Oh no,' Prem said at once; he was shocked when he realized how he had laid himself open to being misunderstood. He knew that, in order to retrieve the situation, he ought to say at once it is for myself I am asking; but before he could get up the courage to say it, Mrs Khanna entered and asked, 'You want more toast?'

Prem immediately brought his hands together in defferential greeting, but she only gave him a sideways and impatient look. She did not care for members of her husband's staff to come into her living-room, and always made this clear when any of them did. She was a short plump woman who wore, even in the house, a lot of gold ornaments and brightly flowered clothes. She looked as opulent and upholstered as her sitting-room, and consequently inspired Prem with the same feeling of shyness.

'You can give me another cup of tea,' Mr Khanna told her.

'Sir,' Prem found himself saying in a croaking voice, 'Mr Sohan Lal is so poor that he cannot even afford to give Mrs Khanna her two rupees eight annas a month for tea.' He saw the look of astonishment on both Mr and Mrs Khanna's faces; Mrs Khanna was staring at him with round eyes, holding the plump teapot with the English cottage on it poised in the air. Prem was astonished himself; he did not know why he was saying so much about Sohan Lal.

Mrs Khanna turned to her husband and said, 'What is he saying?'

'Pour the tea,' he told her.

'Perhaps he is suggesting I make a profit on the money I have to charge for their tea?' Prem was startled by her hostile, even threatening tone. He hung his head and twisted his hands behind his back. He was very much tempted to answer her: they had worked it out long ago and knew that she made a handsome profit on their tea. But if he told her so, she would be very angry with him, and Mr Khanna too would be angry.

'Finest Darjeeling tea I serve to them!' she shouted. 'At what loss to myself every month God only knows!'

Prem looked down at the rug on which he was standing and counted the number of petals to each flower. Why seven, he thought; which flower has seven petals?

'Like a servant I wait on them,' she said; her gold ear-rings were shaking with indignation.

'It is all right,' Mr Khanna said. 'Go now.'

'In what other college,' she demanded from outside the door, 'does

13

the Principal's wife make a slave of herself for her husband's employees?'

After she had gone, there was a short silence between Prem and Mr Khanna, during which they heard her shouting with the same indignation and probably on the same topic in some other room. Mr Khanna said, 'If Mr Sohan Lal wishes to speak with me, perhaps it would be better for him to come himself.'

'No, sir,' Prem said, 'Mr Sohan Lal does not wish to speak with you.' But then he realized that perhaps this was not true; perhaps Sohan Lal did wish to speak to the Principal about something, who knew? Prem felt that the situation was getting rather complicated and that meanwhile he was getting farther and farther away from asking what he had come to ask. He decided to leave aside Sohan Lal and speak out boldly. 'Sir,' he began.

'I think your students must be waiting for you in class,' Mr Khanna said; he finished his tea, wiped his mouth and stood up. Mrs Khanna could still be heard shouting.

'Sir,' said Prem, 'you are yourself a father.'

'It is ten-fifteen.'

'So much?' Prem cried. His students would be waiting. They would be sitting in class making a noise and perhaps Mr Chaddha would pass remarks at them which might disgrace Prem. He begged permission to leave and hurried away. Half-way down the stairs it struck him that he had not asked after all. He hesitated, wondering for a moment whether to go back. But he could not keep his students waiting any longer.

Afterwards he felt very unhappy. He had failed, after all his good resolutions. And what was there so difficult about asking for a rise in salary? It was a very natural thing – everybody, at some time in their life, needed a rise in salary. He should have asked straight out, stood up as a responsible citizen, as a husband and a father, demanding his rights and the rights of his family ... instead of talking about tea and Sohan Lal. When he thought about Sohan Lal, he felt more unhappy still. Perhaps he had even damaged his friend's position; the Principal seemed actually to think that it was Sohan Lal who wanted a rise in salary.

Later, when he saw Sohan Lal in the staffroom, Prem at once had a guilty feeling. He went up to him and said, 'Today I did a very strange thing.'

Sohan Lal smiled. He had an enchanting smile: his teeth were very large and protruding and when he smiled he showed them all, giving an impression of great heartiness.

Prem smiled back at him and said, 'Yes, it was very strange . . .' It seemed quite easy to tell Sohan Lal everything. About Mr Khanna and the rise in salary and the baby and everything. Sohan Lal was bending down to fit his cycle-clips round his trousers. Classes were finished and they were all about to go home. 'May I walk with you a little way?' Prem said.

'You see,' he said, walking beside Sohan Lal who was pushing his cycle along the road, 'I went to speak with the Principal today.' The students were going home too, some walking along the pavement four and five abreast, others jauntily pushing off on shiny new motor-scooters. Some of them called 'Good night, sir!' to Prem and Sohan Lal, in reply to which Sohan Lal waved his hand at them, in a rather embarrassed manner, for like Prem he too was not very good at dealing with the students.

'Things are difficult for me,' Prem said. 'My salary is small – you see, I am married and I pay rent of 45 rupees and my wife is pregnant.' He shot a quick side glance at Sohan Lal: this was the first time he had told anyone, face to face like this, about Indu being pregnant.

Sohan Lal was, as Prem had expected him to be, understanding. He said at once 'You wanted to ask about a rise in salary?'

'What can you do with 175 rupees a month, when your rent alone is 45 rupees?'

'What did he say?'

'It is strange,' Prem said. 'He did not understand.' He shot Sohan Lal another side glance. 'He thought it was you who wanted a rise in salary.'

'I?' Sohan Lal stood still in the road, holding his cycle, and looked at Prem.

'Yes; I told you it was strange.' Both stood and laughed. Students passed them and looked at them in surprise.

'But of course – he is right,' Sohan Lal said. 'I want a rise in salary.'

Prem said, 'I told him you are yourself a father, sir; like that I told him.'

'I pay only 15 rupees rent.'

'Of course, in Mehrauli . . .' Prem said. 'It is a very nice place,' he added quickly. 'Only a little far.'

'It is very far,' Sohan Lal said. 'But where else could I get a place for my whole family for only 15 rupees?'

Prem sighed and said, 'When once one becomes the father of a family, one has to make many sacrifices.'

Sohan Lal smiled in rapturous agreement: this was evidently a subject on which, if he chose, he could speak a lot. But all he said was 'When is your wife expecting?'

'I think in another six months,' Prem said. 'Before that I must have an increase in salary or perhaps find another job. It is very difficult,' he sighed.

'You are still young,' Sohan Lal said. 'Who knows perhaps you will win great success in life – '

'I have only a second-class B.A.'

'Who knows,' Sohan Lal said with a sweet smile. He put one foot on the pedal of his cycle, but before he went, he said unexpectedly, 'Perhaps one day you will come to my house.'

Prem was touched. He very much wanted Sohan Lal to be his friend. He had not yet made any new friends in Delhi and he had not been asked to anyone's house.

He had really only one friend in Delhi. This was Raj, who had gone to college with him in Ankhpur and now had a job in the Ministry of Food. Ever since Prem had come to Delhi, four months ago, they had made a point of meeting on Monday evenings.

Formerly Prem had looked forward all the week to these Monday meetings. He had been so happy to have someone he knew well to talk to: he had confided all his thoughts to Raj, had recalled the old days at Ankhpur, speculated on the whereabout and possible destinies of old friends who had gone their various ways. But he had begun to notice that Raj did not seem to be enjoying these meetings as much as he himself did. He often looked at his watch and, Prem noticed, did not always listen very attentively. And once, while Prem was talking about an old college friend of theirs, he had said with almost a yawn in his voice, 'What is the use of remembering these people? They have gone their way and we have gone ours.' The only two things Raj seemed to be interested in now were his job and his family.

They always met in the same place, by the box-office of the Regal Cinema, not that they ever went into the cinema together, but it was the only place they could think of. Prem was usually the first to arrive. He stood by the little glass window which said Booking Closed and watched the other people standing around in the foyer. These were mostly young men in coloured bush-shirts, who looked about them with lazy eyes while drinking coca-cola or eating potato chips in plastic bags bought from the refreshment bar. When a girl came into the foyer, they straightened themselves and nudged one another and made remarks at which they laughed loudly. The girls always pretended not to notice. Except for the fact that the cinema was larger and there were more people about and everything was smarter and more city-like, it was not much different from what it had been like in Ankhpur: just so had Prem and Raj and their friends stood about in the cinema, eaten potato chips and looked at girls.

But when he saw Raj come into the foyer, Prem realized that now that time was finished for them. Beside these youths in coloured shirts, Raj looked staid and settled and married; he had a preoccupied frown on his face and his shoulders were a little hunched. It was evident that he would never again stand about in cinema foyers and look at girls.

And indeed the first thing he said was, 'This is not a good place to meet. All these boys standing about . . . Loafers,' he said with distaste. They went out together. Prem walked beside his friend in silence, looking away from him for he felt sad that Raj should already have forgotten what was no longer than two years ago.

'Are we going to drink a cup of tea?' Raj asked irritably. In his more downcast moments Prem had already begun to suspect that Raj only met him for the sake of the tea for which it somehow always happened that Prem paid.

They never went into any of the coffee-houses in the main shopping arcade. They had once ventured into one, but had been so overawed by the elaborate decorations and by the many waiters in white uniforms overlooked by a manager in a raw-silk suit that they had quickly gone out again. They felt safer turning down the side-streets and sitting down outside one of the makeshift eating-stalls called the Paris Hotel or Punjab Hotel or Pearl Palace. They always went to a different one because Raj always had some objection to the ones they had been to before. Prem thought that was a pity; he would like to have gone always to the same one, so that they would be known there, as they had been known in the places they had gone to in Ankhpur, and greeted with smiles and a jovial shout of, 'Again the same?'

But now nobody smiled when they sat down outside a stall; only a boy came, wiped the big wooden table and stood waiting for them to order. Raj ordered quite a lot and, as soon as it came, began quickly to eat. 'Today I am in a hurry,' he explained. 'My baby was not well when I left this morning. Maybe I will have to take her to the doctor.'

Prem thought of telling him about his own baby that was on the way. But it had been much easier to tell Sohan Lal. Perhaps because Sohan Lal had not known him when he was young and unmarried and had dreamt about being in love. But Raj knew all that – they had lain together in the grass under a peepul tree and had talked about girls and what it might be like to sleep with one. Now both of them were married to wives their families had chosen for them.

The proprietor of the eating-stall, a big man with a newly shaven skull and a rather dirty vest, was frying fish-cakes; they sizzled in a lake of hot fat while he pushed them about with a stick. The serving-boy squatted in front of the stall and washed dishes in a bucket. A very small puppy with tufts of hair missing ran about wagging its tail and pushing its nose into the dust. There were no customers apart from Prem and Raj. The eating-stall next door had no customers either, and from time to time the two proprietors exchanged scraps of conversation.

Prem said, 'Do you remember Kakaji's?' Kakaji's was the eating-stall they had gone to in Ankhpur: Kakaji gave credit to all the students for biscuits and tea. If any student ran up too large a bill Kakaji went and complained to the Principal of the college, who was Prem's father. Each time the boys passed a resolution to boycott Kakaji's, but the proprietors of the other eating-stalls in Ankhpur would not give them credit, so they always came back.

Raj, chewing with bulging cheeks, made a noncommittal sound, which made it clear that his interest in Kakaji's had long since evaporated. This was not surprising, for Prem asked the same question every week. Indeed, Prem himself did not feel so much interest in the subject any more, and only touched on it for something to say. Not that there were not plenty of other things which he would have preferred saying; but he could not get over his shyness with Raj.

'Nice smell,' said Raj, referring to the fish-cakes.

Prem swallowed hard and led up to the subject at present closest to his heart: 'Today I went to see my Principal.'

'I don't usually eat fish at this time of day, otherwise I might try some.'

'Things are rather difficult for me now,' Prem said. 'You see, I pay 45 rupees rent – '

'I also pay 25 rupees. And don't forget I have a baby to support.'

'As a matter of fact – ' Prem slowly began. His ears grew hot.

'You have no idea how expensive a baby can be. It drinks so much milk and then it needs clothes – '

'I know. That is why I went to see the Principal. But I don't think he understood what I meant to say.'

'It is fantastic how quickly a baby can grow out of its clothes. And as soon as it starts walking, there are shoes also and those go even quicker.' Raj spoke with the same animation on this subject as he had once spoken about love and girls and Kakaji.

Prem said, 'I shall have to ask him again. Next time I shall say right out I want more pay.'

'You are lucky not to be in Goverment service. In Government service whom can you ask? Can you go and say Mr Government, I want more pay?' Raj was pleased with this joke and leant back to laugh. A young beggar-woman with a pretty face and merry eyes shining out of dirt and rags and a baby sleeping in her arms, approached them and began her professional whine: 'Sahib,' she said, holding out one cupped hand. Raj motioned her away: 'You will get nothing here,' he said.

'I may have to look for another job,' Prem said.

'Of course,' Raj said, 'Government service has many other compensations. For instance, there is a pension and provident fund' –

'It would be good if I could get a job with Government.'

'Look at my child, how hungry he is,' the beggarwoman said.

'A Government job is a safe job. Nobody can tell you get out – '

'For four days I have put nothing in my stomach.' She patted it vigorously and looked at them with laughing eyes.

'Go away!' Raj said, and the proprietor also shouted, 'Get out!'

'You are my mother and my father,' the beggar-woman said, edging nearer. Prem put his hand in his pocket and gave her a coin. She inspected it critically, then hitched up the sleeping child and moved off without further comment.

'You are a fool to give,' Raj said. Prem shrugged; he too knew he was a fool, but somehow he felt better after giving. 'Wait till you have a family, then you will not be so free with your money,' Raj said.

'As a matter of fact – '

'Now I must go. This morning my baby was sick.'

The serving-boy came to take their money. 'How much?' Raj inquired, his hand pretending to grope towards his pocket. Prem drew out the money and, while he paid, Raj turned round in his chair to where the beggar-woman was now begging at the next stall; he said to her, 'What, you are here again?' in an angry voice. When the paying was over, he turned back and told Prem, 'Again you have paid, this is very bad.' Prem said, 'Then next Monday?'

He was surprised to find Indu downstairs on the Seigals' front porch. What surprised him further was that she was happy and smiling; she never looked like that at home. The Seigals too were smiling. Mr Seigal stood with his legs apart and his hands laid on his big belly; he was looking down on Indu with great benevolence, saying, 'Why don't you come more often?' and when he saw Prem he shouted, 'Why do you keep your wife locked up all the time?'

'I?' said Prem and was about to start defending himself when he realized it was a joke. Then he hung his head and shuffled his feet and shyly smiled.

'You must both come,' said Mrs Seigal. 'What is the use of sitting by yourselves up there?' She was crocheting, hooking the needle with great dexterity. From time to time she spread out and flattened the finished part and looked at it critically. Indu said, 'How beautiful' and fingered it. 'It is a tablecloth,' said Mrs Seigal; and added, 'With things like this we keep busy.'

'While we men slave to bring home the money,' said Mr Seigal to Prem with a manly guffaw which Prem tried but failed to echo. He never felt at ease with the Seigals. For one thing, they were his landlords, and remembrance of the 45 rupees rent he was obliged to pay them in the first week of every month made a really hearty relationship difficult. And then their way of life was so much more expansive than anything he had been brought up to; Somehow he could not help feeling a tinge of disapproval at their nightly card-parties, the lights and the noise and the radio, the whisky, the cups of tea and the plates of sweetmeats so freely circulated. He did not think that such ease was conducive to a really noble life.

Mr Seigal patted his hands against the sides of his belly and asked Prem, 'so how are you getting on?' in an offhand tone of bonhomie which did not require any answer. Prem, however, felt very much tempted to reply. The thought of his increasing responsibilities was so pressing to him that he would have liked to share it with anyone who showed even the slightest interest in his concerns.

'You can come and sit with me and we will both crochet a quilt together,' Mrs Seigal was telling Indu, who smiled and looked happy at the prospect. Prem caught a glimpse of her face out of the corner of his eye and it struck him that, when she smiled, she was really quite pretty. At the same time another thought occurred to him and that was that she had told the Seigals – or at least Mrs Seigal who would, in her turn, have told her husband – that she was pregnant. In which case, all the time that he was standing here, they knew what it was he did with Indu; perhaps they were even thinking about it. Mr Seigal was looking at him in a shrewd, knowing, amused way, which might very well mean that he *was* thinking about it.

'Work to do . . . Papers to correct,' Prem muttered, making a hasty departure. Indu followed reluctantly behind. The smile had gone from her face, giving way to a look of disappointment. She even sighed, softly but nevertheless enough to irritate Prem. He said, 'What is the matter?' in a tone of voice which dared her to say anything *was* the matter.

'Nothing,' Indu softly and obediently sighed, with her face turned aside from him.

'When you are with them you smile. Here you only sigh.' To this she had no reply, and her silence encouraged him to probe his grievance further. 'I work so hard all day,' he reminded her, 'and when I come home, there you sit and sigh.'

She was squatting on the floor, picking at the hem of her sari. He looked down at her meek bent head. 'What is the matter?' he said. 'Are you unwell?' Her head shook. 'Then why do you sigh?' He paced the room in some agitation. 'It is I who should sigh. If you know how many worries I have . . .' He wanted to add 'because of you' but kindness restrained him.

'What is a salary of only 175 rupees? It is very little, it is nothing. Our rent alone costs us 45 rupees a month.' He paced some more and ran his hand through his hair. 'Just think,' he cried, '45 rupees!'

Suddenly she said, 'Why don't you ask Mr Seigal to make your rent less?'

He was so surprised that she should make any suggestion – let alone such a sensible one – that he stood and stared at her. This confused her, and she bent her head lower and continued to pick at the hem of her sari. 'What?' Prem said. 'What did you say?' hoping that she had something else sensible to bring forward.

But she would not say it again. Probably she thought he would laugh at her or scold her. She jumped up and ran into the kitchen, where she promptly began to shout at the servant-boy.

Prem followed her and said, 'You think he would?'

'You call this clean?' she was shouting, thrusting a saucepan under the boy's nose. The boy stood quite still and stared into the distance with a patient look.

'You think he would reduce our rent, if I asked him?'

'Even to clean saucepans I have to teach you!' Indu shouted.

'Well, answer me,' Prem insisted.

'How do I know?' she said. 'There is a letter for you. It is lying on the bed.'

It was from his mother, but he did not at once open it. Instead he lay down on the bed and thought about what Indu had said.

The bed was their only really good piece of furniture. It had been a present from Indu's uncle and was a large double bed of shiny teak; the headrest was decorated with two carved cherubs who had their arms clasped about one another's necks. The poky crooked little bedroom was really not good enough for this magnificent bed. Prem was very proud of it and liked to lie on it, even in the daytime. He lay there and thought about how he would ask Mr Seigal to reduce his rent.

Still thinking about this, he ripped open his mother's letter. He read 'My dearest son' and after that, from the expressions of happiness and gratitude to God, realized that this letter was in reply to the one he had sent announcing Indu's pregnancy. He finished reading in haste and some embarrassment, but was glad to find in the end that his mother intended to come and visit them. It would be nice to have her here: she would make the flat more comfortable and homelike, and also perhaps she would teach Indu how to cook the dishes he liked.

Indu stood in the doorway and said shyly, 'I also had a letter today.' She was holding it out to him.

'Who is it from?'

'It is from my mother.' He did not take it, though she was still holding it out to him; instead he said, 'What does she write?'

After a short pause, Indu said in a low voice, 'She wants me to come home.'

Prem had no comment to make. It did not, he thought, greatly matter to him whether she stayed or went.

Indu confessed, 'I wrote to her about . . .' and 'Yes, yes,' said Prem in some irritation. 'That is why she wants me to come home,' Indu said.

'My mother is coming to visit us,' Prem said.

22

After thinking this over for a while, Indu said, 'Then she will be able to look after you here when I am gone.'

'How can you go away when my mother is coming to visit us?'

'Why not?' Indu inquired. The innocence of her voice as she asked this made him quite angry. He shouted, 'What do you mean why not? Have you no sense?' She looked at him with her eyes wide in amazement. He had never before shouted at her.

Now that he had started, he rather felt like shouting some more. But he thought of the Seigals downstairs and the servant-boy in the kitchen, and so changed to a fierce whisper. 'Don't you understand that my mother will be offended?' he hissed, supporting himself on one elbow as he lay on the bed and leaning towards her.

'Why are you whispering?' she asked.

'How stupid you are – do you want everyone to hear us quarrelling?'

'I am not quarrelling.'

He lay back again, feeling rather defeated. How stupid she is, he thought; one could not even argue with her.

Indu said, 'My mother wants me to come home.'

'But how can you, when *my* mother is coming?' He tried to sound terribly reasonable but only succeeded in sounding annoyed.

'All girls go home when they are . . .'

'Not at the beginning. Only in the end, when their time has come.'

'Yes, at the beginning also.' She was pouting. She pushed out her full lower lip and half closed her lids over her eyes. Her eyes were her best feature; they were very large and took up most of her face which was small though set on a long neck. 'And my mother wants me to come,' she said. Her voice too had turned sulky.

'If your mother knew that my mother was coming to visit us, she would not want you to come.' He kept looking at her. Really, he thought, she is not bad-looking. Yet he remembered that when he had first seen her, he had been disappointed.

'Yes, she would want. I told you, all girls go home when they are in this condition.'

'You talk as if it is my fault that you are – ' Before he could finish, she had asked, 'Then whose fault is it?' This struck him as definitely indelicate. He frowned, for he did not like girls to be indelicate. They should be remote and soulful; like Goddesses they should be. 'It is not nice to talk like that,' he reproved her.

'What did I say? Only what is true.'

He would have explained to her that it is not always right for a girl to say what is true; but what use was explaining? A girl should understand these things by herself.

'How can I say no to my mother?'

'If you explain to her that your mother-in-law is coming to visit you – '

'She will say what is your mother-in-law against your own mother?' And before Prem could even contemplate an answer, she shouted, 'And she would be right to say so!' and withdrew quickly into the sitting-room.

Prem continued to lie on the bed. He felt sorry for himself, to be married to a wife who was not only quite different from what he had wished and hoped for, but who also opposed him in his wishes. He strained his ears, trying to hear what was going on in the sitting-room. He heard nothing except the servant-boy clattering in the kitchen, but he could guess that Indu was sitting there crying. He had seen tears in her eyes when she had left the room so hastily. It made him uncomfortable to think of her crouching alone in there, crying quietly to herself. She always cried very quietly. He had by accident discovered her on two occasions; when she had seen him, she had pretended to be blowing her nose.

He wondered whether other people's wives behaved like this too. It was strange, when he and Raj had been unmarried, they had discussed everything, their most secret thoughts; but now they could talk freely about nothing, least of all about their own wives whom they never as much as referred to. Yet Prem longed to talk to someone about his married state. It was such a new and unknown thing for him, he felt he could not deal with it. How, for instance, was he to deal with Indu crying to herself in the next room? He began to feel like crying himself; already a tear was trembling on his cheek. He brushed it aside with his hand and the feel of it made him want to cry more. He felt so alone and lonely, shut up in this small ugly flat with Indu who cried by herself in the sitting-room while he had to lie and cry by himself in the bedroom.

If at least he had been happy in his work. But he felt just as alone and lonely in the college as he did at home. He stood in front of his class and talked to them about present and past participles; and though he tried to feel interested in what he was saying, he could not help being bored. His students, he could see, were not taking notes as industriously as they should have been; some of them were scribbling drawings on their notebooks, others leaning back and looking up at the ceiling; others were holding conversation together and not even bothering to keep to a respectful whisper. While in the other half of the classroom, Mr Chaddha's students were taut with attention, their heads bent all in a row over their notebooks, while Mr Chaddha piped forcefully and with many emphatic gestures about trade in British India. Prem felt dispirited at this difference between his own and Mr Chaddha's half of the classroom. It occurred to him that really he ought to try and assert himself, and with this in mind he called in a sharp voice to one of the students who was talking, 'Please pay attention to my lecture.'

The student stopped talking and looked at him in surprise; the others also stopped talking, and those who had been looking at the ceiling looked down again. They were all now staring at Prem and evidently expecting something more from him. 'A vast network of railways was flung from coast to coast!' Mr Chaddha declaimed, sweeping one hand through the air. Prem cleared his throat and said in a voice considerably less severe than before. 'In class one must always pay attention to what the teacher says.' Then he hastily carried on with illustrations of present and past participles. His students relaxed again and returned to their own private preoccupations.

Afterwards he sat in the staffroom and waited for Sohan Lal to finish eating. Sohan Lal sat perched on the end of a little bench with his back turned shyly to the room; he ate quickly and furtively, in a very humble way. It was not until he had quite finished and was packing up his tiffin-carrier again that Prem went and sat next to him. 'I have been thinking what we were talking the other day,' Prem said. He said this only as an opening; it was not only what they had been talking about the other day that he wanted to discuss, but many other things as well.

Sohan Lal radiated his big smile of protruding teeth. Nothing could have been more encouraging to Prem to go on talking, to talk about everything that was on his mind. There was so much he wanted to say. 'Things are very difficult for me,' he began. Sohan Lal became serious and clicked his tongue in sympathy.

'You see,' said Prem, 'I have not been married long . . .'

He stopped, shy not of Sohan Lal but of the place in which they were. Mr Chaddha was looking through some students' papers, with a frown on his face; from time to time he shook his head and said,

25

'Senseless boys.' Two other staff members were having an argument about the Socialist party. 'I suppose it is like this for everybody?' Prem inquired of Sohan Lal, forgetting that he had not yet made clear what he meant by 'like this'.

'Life is often difficult,' said Sohan Lal encouragingly.

'You see, I am all alone here,' Prem said. 'My family live in Ankhpur and I have no one to help me.' This sounded so pathetic, even to himself, that he at once felt very sad. He said, 'Yes, you are right, life is difficult.'

The Principal came striding into the staff-room and said, 'Good morning, gentlemen.' He always addressed his staff, when several of them were gathered together, as 'gentlemen'; this lent dignity to the school, giving the impression that he employed real professors and paid them a high salary.

'I am inviting you all to a tea-party,' Mr Khanna announced. There was a moment's silence and then Mr Chaddha piped up, 'Thank you, sir', and rubbed his hands to demonstrate delight. The others, including Prem, also echoed 'Thank you' in voices they tried to make joyful.

Mr Khanna looked benevolent: 'Social contact between our members of staff must be stimulated,' he explained. 'Only so will our college thrive and flourish.' Mr Chaddha said, 'Hear, hear.' 'We must be,' said Mr Khanna, 'like one big family. Mrs Khanna has kindly consented to serve tea and other refreshments.' Another staff-member also said, 'Hear, hear.' 'It is on Sunday week at four-thirty p.m. sharp,' Mr Khanna said. 'Of course, ladies are also invited.' 'Very charming,' said Mr Chaddha.

'He means we must bring our wives?' Prem asked Sohan Lal, after the Principal had gone. This was a new worry for him: how could he bring Indu? She would not know what to do or say, and perhaps bring disgrace on him. 'I don't know whether it will be possible for me to bring my wife,' he said.

'Ladies are usually very shy,' Sohan Lal said.

'It is not that alone,' said Prem. He thought of words in which he could explain how difficult it would be for him to bring Indu. I hardly know her, he wanted to say; how can I bring someone I hardly know to such an important tea-party? Yet it seemed a strange thing to say about one's own wife especially after he had already confessed to Sohan Lal that Indu was pregnant.

In the evening, on their way home, he talked rather more freely.

'You see,' he said, 'it is not very long ago that I was a student living in my parent's house.' Sohan Lal nodded. 'I had no worries there at all, except only that I should pass in my examinations.' Sohan Lal was pushing his cycle along the edge of the road; he was looking down at the gutter, but his head was slightly inclined towards Prem which gave him the appearance of listening with great attention and sympathy.

'Everything was so different then!' cried Prem.

'Yes,' said Sohan Lal, quite sadly,' when we are young and have no responsibilities life is very beautiful.'

'Suddenly there are so many responsibilities,' Prem said. 'For instance, I never had to worry about money – of course, I never had much money but my father gave me an allowance and that was enough for tea and biscuits and cinema sometimes . . .'

'When we are young, so many things cost nothing.'

'That is true,' Prem said. 'We often went on picnics and that did not cost anything because our mothers gave us food to take and we had a very jolly time though we did not spend anything.'

'In our youth the sky is blue and the trees are green and the birds sing. What worries can we have when things are like that?'

'Yes, yes,' Prem cried and he stood still in his excitement, 'it was exactly like that! I remember our picnics . . .'

'Good night, sir!' called a group of students. They swaggered down the road, confident, idle young men in good clothes, with their arms slung around one another's shoulders, joking as they went.

Prem looked after them and said, 'Of course, I know all things must come to an end.' And then he added, 'If only it did not happen so quickly.'

Yet he found himself quite anxious to go home. This was a new sensation for him: he had never yet looked forward to going back to Indu. Nor was he exactly looking forward to her now; what he wanted was to take up yesterday's discussion with her and make sure that she was not going to her father's house. He did not tell himself that he wanted to quarrel with her; all he told himself was that the subject really must be gone into again.

As he walked up the stairs, he heard her singing. She was squatting in the kitchen, kneading dough very deftly and quickly, so that her bangles jingled. When she saw him, she stopped singing and continued her work with her head lowered.

'Where is the servant?' Prem said.

'He has gone out.'

'He is always out,' Prem said disapprovingly.

'There is not much work. We don't really need a servant.'

'Of course we need a servant,' Prem said. After all, he was the son of a Principal of a college and himself a professor, a man of education and some standing: it was not right that his wife should scour pots and wash floors. He felt annoyed that she should fail to realize this, and he at once vented his annoyance: 'What do you think people will say if they come here and find we have no servant?'

'But nobody comes,' Indu pointed out. He made a sound of impatience. How completely she missed his point! She really seemed to be rather stupid.

'If someone comes or does not come,' he said with dignity, 'we must keep up our honour. Would you eat dirt from the road even though no one saw you?' He delivered this last allegory with some triumph, but it appeared she had not understood. At any rate she gave him no reply.

He wandered into the sitting-room but as she did not follow him, he was soon back again to ask her, 'Did you have another letter from your mother today?' to which she only shook her head.

'I think my mother will be coming to stay with us soon,' he said.

To this too she had no reply to give. He wondered whether her silence meant that she had acquiesced in his wishes or whether it was a silence of obstinacy and smouldering defiance. He tried to scrutinize her face, but she had already turned it away from him. This rather confirmed his suspicion that her silence meant defiance. He knitted his brows and wondered how to deal with the situation.

He lacked a precedent for it not only in his own life but also in that of his parents. As far as he was aware, his mother had not been in the habit of defying his father. Of course, his father had been a very important man – the Principal of Ankhpur College – so that when he uttered an opinion everybody had stood silent and listened with respect. And Prem's mother had been the most respectful of all. She had prefaced all her remarks to Prem and his sisters with 'Your father says', and to outsiders she said, 'The Principal says.' In the house everybody had had to tiptoe past his study, and at mealtimes he always had some special dish cooked in which no one else had been allowed to share. Prem had sometimes envied him his position of comfort and dignity and had looked forward to being married himself so that he could occupy a similar one. But Indu, it seemed, was not aware of the privileges due to him.

28

Raj must have been through all this with his wife. He wished he could have talked to him about it, the way they used to talk together before they had been married. Raj would know better than Sohan Lal, who was a much older man and had been married a long time and so had probably forgotten what it was like in the beginning. How ridiculous, Prem thought, to feel shy with Raj; next time, he decided, he would talk to him quite freely. They would sit and have tea in one of the little eating-stalls they usually frequented and fully discuss their matrimonial troubles. Nothing, Prem promised himself, would be left unsaid.

But on the next Monday Raj failed to turn up. Prem stood by the box-office in the cinema and waited for him for a whole hour and a half. He felt rather awkward standing there waiting, and was even afraid that the manager might send someone to ask what he wanted. To make himself less suspicious, he wandered round from time to time to look at the pictures of forthcoming attractions, and once he bought a packet of potato crisps from the refreshment bar. As usual, there were many young men standing around, talking and joking together and looking at girls. They made Prem feel lonely and even a little elderly. This feeling was heightened when one group of young men turned out to be his students. 'Good evening, sir,' they said, politely enough, but Prem noticed that when they thought he could no longer see them, they nudged one another and laughed. He remembered that Raj and he and their other friends had laughed and nudged in the same way when they had happened to meet one of their professors outside the college.

He left the cinema and went out into the street. There were the usual evening crowds, and they made him feel more lonely than ever, Everyone, except himself, seemed to have a companion and a destination. He crossed over to walk in the round of green in the centre. Here it was quieter. A few clerks sat on the grass, eating hot gram out of paper cones, and there was an ice-cream man with a yellow van and a solitary boy slid despondently down the chute. Prem sat down on a bench and watched an elderly Parsee gentleman in a black stove-pipe hat resting on an opposite bench. When he was tired of looking at him, he looked at the sky instead which, since it was sunset time, was a very delicate pink with streaks of flaring orange across it. How beautiful, Prem thought, how beautiful is Nature. He felt he ought to elaborate that sentiment to himself, and get something really noble and significant out of it. All this beauty has been created for man to enjoy, he thought; and would perhaps have gone further in searching out philosophy and deep meaning, when at this moment another voice said behind him, 'What beautiful sunsets you have in India.'

Prem turned and saw a young man, a European, with a big head and rimless spectacles. 'I was also admiring, like you,' he said, nodding with a smile towards the sky. 'I was thinking how much beauty is there in India, how much colour is there, it is all so nice – but this is the country where people renounce the flesh and think only of the Spirit!' Prem stared at him. 'It is marvellous,' said the young man. 'I may sit with you?' He flung himself down on the grass at Prem's feet though there was plenty of room on the bench. He said, 'Only think – in this country where everything is beautiful, the sunset and the fruit and the women, here you call it all Illusion! How do you say – Maya?' Prem said, 'Yes, Maya,' though he was not quite sure. He could not take his eyes off this young man, who seemed to him very strange.

'What is this Maya? Why do you say so? Explain me, please.' He folded his arms and looked at Prem very challengingly. Prem began to panic a little, for he was not sure how or what he was expected to explain. But the young man did not really wait for an answer. He unfolded his arms again and called in a loud joyful voice, 'How I love your India!' His pale eyes behind the rimless spectacles shone with happiness, he showed moist colourless gums in a blissful smile. 'For me it is all one big feast!'

Prem felt called upon to make some comment. He was proud to hear a foreigner speak so highly of India, it raised all his patriotism. 'Since Independence,' he said, 'we have made great strides forward. For instance, our second Five Year Plan – '

'Everything is so spiritual – we can wash off our dirty materialism when we come here to your India. Off with it!' and he started quite literally scrubbing at his arms and then at his neck with great vigour.

'There are our new steel plants,' said Prem. 'Six million tons of steel – '

'It is such an old country and yet fresh – oh, my God, fresh like a newborn child!' He wrung his hands in ecstasy and smiled. Then suddenly he introduced himself: 'I am Hans Loewe.' He held out a large hand but before Prem could shake it, he withdrew it again and said, 'No, like this', and joined his hands together in front of his face in Indian salute: 'Namaste,' he said with a very strange accent. 'Loewe means lion – I am Hans the Lion.' He roared like one and then slapped his knee in laughter. Prem laughed with him, out of politeness.

'Now we will drink a cup of coffee together,' said Hans, 'and talk a little.' Prem followed him at once. The old Parsee was still sitting quietly on his bench and the clerks had bought bars of vanilla ice-cream on sticks from the man with the yellow van. But Prem did not even look at them. He was excited and felt his evening, which only a moment ago had been so empty and idle, to be full of adventure.

Hans led him into one of the coffee-houses in the main arcade. It was crowded, and waiters rushed about leaning sideways under the weight of trays; there was a lot of noise, people talked loudly and laughed, the waiters shouted orders into the kitchen and a row of fans whirred from the ceiling. But Prem did not feel shy or afraid, as he would have done if he had come with Raj. He had confidence in Hans, who indeed seemed to have a lot of confidence in himself. He moved forward like one elbowing his way through a crowd, in a lumbering forceful manner which soon found them an empty table. It was in a far dark corner and they sat there like lovers, side by side on a red sofa with stains on it.

Hans said, 'Now you will ask me, how did I first come to this marvellous India?' Prem nodded. 'I will tell you,' said Hans, with a relish that showed it was a good story and one that he liked to tell.

But while he was getting ready to tell it, moistening his lips by running his tongue round them and settling himself in his seat, Prem said, 'I am Hindi lecturer in Khanna Private College. My father was Principal of Ankhpur College.'

'Ah,' said Hans, 'You are intellectual. I have great respect for the intellectuals. Now I will tell you. You see, one night I had a dream Yes, you heard right – a dream. You are laughing?' Prem shook his head. He could not keep his eyes off Hans. How ugly he is, he thought. Hans' face had been turned a pale red by the sun and here and there, in odd places round his nose and forehead, the skin was peeling; his hair had been shaved so close that all that remained of it were tiny ends of blond bristle sparsely covering a big bumpy skull.

'Yes,' said Hans, 'what brought me here was a dream. You see, one night I was sleeping in my bed.' He shut his eyes and laid his head to rest sideways on his hands to illustrate his sleep. 'Seven thousand miles away from your India, in Frankfurt, Germany. That is a long way, isn't it? Yes, but in a dream that is nothing. What does it matter, in a dream, seven miles, seven hundred miles, seven thousand miles?'

Prem shook his head to signify that it did not matter. 'So in my dream what do I see suddenly? I see India. Yes, your marvellous India I see. I see a palm tree and a temple. Under this palm tree who is sitting? Please bring me whipped cream with my coffee,' he told the waiter. 'In Germany we drink coffee with cream whipped thick.'

Prem said, 'For good coffee you must go to South India.'

'Who is sitting under the palm tree?' Hans said, raising an admonitory forefinger and looking sternly at Prem, who at once changed the expression on his face to one of deep wonder and concentration. 'It is a holy man. What you call a sadhu. Right?'

'Yes, sadhu,' Prem said.

'He is naked except for one cloth. He is sitting with his legs crossed under him. He is looking at me. His eyes, oh his eyes!' Hans called, raising his hands in rapture. A group of stout businessmen in transparent bush-shirts turned round to look at him from an adjacent table. 'Such pity, such kindness there is in those eyes. Such love. And they are looking at me. Yes, at me, Hans Loewe'; he indicated himself with his forefinger. 'And what do they say to me, those marvellous eyes?' The businessmen turned back again, shrugging at one another, and continued their conversation. Prem wished Hans would not talk so loudly.

'Their message is simple,' said Hans. 'It is only this: "Come, Hans";' and he smiled, showing his tiny teeth and his gums. 'Yes, only come, Hans. But it is enough. I take the rucksack on the back, I am here. Now tell me about you.' He folded his hands and looked at Prem with an expression of patient attention.

But Prem had already told about his father being Principal of Ankhpur College and himself a lecturer at Khanna Private College. What more could he tell him? He flushed slightly and then brought it out hastily: 'I have been married four months.'

Hans said, 'Is your wife beautiful?'

Prem bent his head and toyed furiously with his coffee-spoon. He did not know how anyone could come to put such an indecent question.

'Indian women are all so beautiful,' Hans said. 'When I walk in the street, I fall in love at least one hundred times.' Then he cried: 'And with such women, you renounce the flesh!' Prem said 'Sh' and looked round apprehensively. 'Marvellous!' Hans shouted. 'To practise abstinence when there are such women with such – '

'Perhaps we should ask for the bill?'

'You are in a hurry to go home to your new wife?' Hans said with a hearty laugh.

'No, I . . .' Prem hastily raised his coffee-cup and pretended to drink from it, though it was quite empty.

'I am making jokes. You will get used to me, I always make jokes.' Prem forced a laugh. 'Well, but we are friends now? You will come to visit me?' He snatched at the coat of a passing waiter, who however did not stop. 'This is where I live,' he said, writing it down on the menu. 'You can come on Wednesday at six?'

When the bill came, Prem, who had been conditioned by Raj, at once offered to pay it. But Hans said, 'We are friends now?' Prem nodded, feeling shy though pleased. 'Friends share everything,' Hans said. 'They share even bills.' He laughed and slapped money on the table. 'Here is my half.' Prem drew out his money. 'Marvellous!' Hans shouted. 'This is called fifty-fifty.' He held out his hand but, again, before Prem could shake it, he withdrew it, saying, 'No, like this', and joined his hands in Indian salute. 'Namaste,' he said in his strange accent.

Prem was tremendously excited. All the time he thought about his new friend. When he got home, he hoped to meet the Seigals and be drawn into conversation with them, in the course of which he could mention that he had won the friendship of a German boy called Hans Loewe. But they were inside the house – he could hear them talking with friends – so he climbed up the stairs and found Indu counting out their laundry to the washerman. All their sheets and towels were spread over the floor of the sitting-room; Indu was saying, 'What do you use for washing clothes – cow-dung?' which annoyed Prem because it was so very unrefined. The washerman grinned with pleasure and began to protest how he used only the finest soap. 'Why don't you count the clothes in the bedroom?' Prem said irritably, so they finished in a hurry. When the washerman had gone, Prem said, 'Why do you talk with him like that?'

'Should I fill the water for your bath?' Indu said.

'You are the lady of the household, you must behave with dignity and win everyone's respect.' Indu turned away her face, but Prem noticed that she had covered her mouth with her hand and was giggling behind it; he could tell from the way she hunched up her shoulders. So he said in an injured tone, 'It is nothing to laugh at.'

'I am not laughing,' Indu said; her voice sounded very stifled and she immediately put her hand over her mouth again.

'You are no longer a girl in your father's house,' he reproached her. He suspected that it was her father's house that was responsible for her unrefined behaviour. In the short while that he had known her family – that is to say, during the days of wedding celebrations – he had noticed that they were rather loud in their behaviour. Indu's mother and her aunts were always shouting, either with laughter or with anger, and her sisters sang and giggled and played a lot of practical jokes. He had felt very uncomfortable among them and had been glad when it was all over.

'And how do I look,' he said, 'with a wife who doesn't know how to behave with dignity!' That reminded him of Mr Khanna's tea-party. He realized that he must prepare her from now on and start impressing upon her the way in which she was expected to behave. 'There is one very important matter,' he said and turned round to find that she had left the room.

He followed her into the kitchen. 'Why do you go away when I am speaking with you?'

'I thought you had finished speaking,' she said. She said it demurely enough, yet he could not help suspecting that she was laughing at him. The idea of a wife laughing at her husband! He deliberately called to mind his mother's deferential attitude towards his father in order to feel more poignantly how Indu was failing him.

'Of course I have not finished,' he said sternly. 'There are many important matters a husband and wife have to discuss together.' He could not quite define how it seemed to him that Indu was laughing at him. Her eyes were modestly lowered and she appeared intent on preparing dough for parathas. But the way her hands moved so swiftly and her bangles jingled and a strand of hair which had escaped from her big coil fluttered merrily on her cheek as she kneaded and pounded the dough: somehow her whole figure expressed laughter. He wanted to be angry with her, and yet also he wanted to laugh with her. He very much needed someone to laugh with and to talk to and confide in. How wonderful if it could have been Indu, with whom he lived and who lay beside him at night. He could tell her everything about the college and his feelings and experiences. He could tell her about Hans Loewe. He wanted very much to tell her about Hans Loewe.

But instead he spoke sternly again: 'It is a wife's duty to share all her husband's worries.' She wiped a strand of hair from her face; she wiped it away with her upper arm, for her hands were full of dough.

34

As she did so, he could not help noticing the soft skin on the inside of her arm. 'I have so many worries, but you take no interest in them at all,' he said; his voice had changed to being querulous instead of stern. He wished she would lift her arm again, but was so ashamed of the wish that he would hardly admit it to himself.

She said, 'What do I understand of these things?'

'You must learn to understand. A wife must help her husband and be a support to him.' Was she going to laugh again? He saw her lip tremble and her head turn farther away from him. How ridiculous she was; like a child. He looked at the nape of her long neck and noticed how very fine strands of hair curled there in a most childlike manner.

'Next Sunday you will have to come with me to the college,' he said. 'The Principal is giving a tea-party for staff members and their wives.'

Her head turned back quickly towards him. Her eyes were stretched wide open – obviously she was very startled. 'It is to stimulate social contact between the whole staff,' Prem said. He was rather pleased with the effect his news had on her. 'The Principal wants us all to be like one big family.'

'How can I go?'

'Why not?'

'I – ' She stopped, and laughed, but it was a tearful laugh.

'Of course you must come. Mr Khanna said specially that it was very important for all wives to come.' On this uncompromising note he left her and went to lie on their big bed, supporting his head against the cherubs.

She followed him after a while and suggested timidly, 'You could say I was sick.' Her hands were still full of dough.

'Why should I say you are sick?'

'Then they would not expect me to come.'

'But I told you – you must come! You must accompany me and make a good impression.' A look of anguish appeared on her face; then she turned and walked away with her head lowered. He wished it were night and all dark and she beside him in the bed. He felt ashamed of the wish and got up and had a bath in cold water, trying not to think of her.

The baby did not occur to him very often. When he thought of it, he thought of it more in connection with money troubles and how its arrival would necessitate a higher salary or a lower rent or, better still, both. Only sometimes he wondered vaguely whether it would be a boy or a girl. Though one morning, as he passed a boisterous group of students on their way to the college, it occurred to him that he might have a son who would grow up to be like these boys. The thought did nothing much to him except to create new money worries. He had a fair idea how much these boys must be costing their parents. The Khanna Private College was not cheap. Mr Khanna specialized in boys from well-off families who were not clever enough to get admission into the better colleges. He kept them for a year or so, during which time he ostensibly trained them to get past the admission tests. That most of them did so was perhaps due less to their own hard work than to Mr Khanna's contacts, which were very good. Meanwhile the boys had a pleasant time. They wore stylish clothes, travelled fast on motor-scooters, paid frequent visits to cinemas and restaurants. Some of them even had girls.

Prem could not help envying his students. He hoped his son would grow up like them, healthy and confident and rich. Though this last was, in view of his own salary, hardly possible. It made him feel sad to think that he would not be able to give his son a motor-scooter; and, as usual, when he was sad or thoughtful, he became philosophical. God has drawn a circle round each of us, he thought, and we cannot step over the line that He has drawn. It seemed to him a good thought, which he would like to have shared with his students.

He was standing in front of his class, analysing a sentence for them into its component parts, and was regretfully aware that they were, as usual, bored. Probably they were thinking of what they were going to do in the evening. Prem wished he could have stopped talking about subject and predicate and discussed other, more important, matters with them. The bored look would disappear from their faces and they would lean forward in their seats and eagerly listen to him. He would tell them about how only a short time ago he too had been a student like them, but how now he was married and was about to have a son whom he would have to support and send to college. He was sure they would be sympathetic and interested. Though, in their pursuit of pleasure, they gave an impression both of frivolity and arrogance, he knew from the compositions they wrote for him that they were also capable of sentiment. He suspected that they too spent long hours lying on their backs with their arms clasped behind their heads, as he and Raj had done, to discuss or simply meditate on important aspects of life. It was on that level that he wished to appeal to them. He was sure that there he could establish a contact with them which as a teacher he had quite failed to do.

It seemed to him that he was failing in everything – as a husband and as a teacher. His father had been so successful in both capacities. But Prem felt he had no vocation for either. He did not know what he did have a vocation for. The only thing he had done successfully so far was to have been a student who lived in his father's house and went for walks with his friends. He still felt that that alone was his true condition, even though he had been married now and employed in Khanna Private College for some months. It was as if all the time he were waiting to go home to be looked after and cared for by his family.

Yet he wanted very much to be a successful man. His father, both as a Principal and a father, had always impressed upon him the importance of being a successful man. 'You must strive, strive and strive again!' his father had said, looking very impressive as he said it, with his jaw set and his hand striking down emphatically upon the table. Prem had taken this as referring mainly to his examinations, and he had been glad to be able to pass them. But now he realized that that had after all not been the end of striving, and that something more was required of him.

In the staffroom he listened to the other lecturers discussing Sunday's tea-party, as they had been doing ever since the Principal had announced it. Mr Chaddha, glancing up from his book for a moment, interposed, 'I am looking forward to a pleasant afternoon. Mrs Chaddha has also consented to be present.' He cleared his throat, crossed his legs and again concentrated his attention with raised eyebrow on his book. Though he was so small and thin and birdlike, there was something very authoritative about him, and he radiated a confidence which Prem could not help wishing he possessed. He realized that he should be looking up to Mr Chaddha and trying to emulate him; and he wondered why it was that he should feel more drawn towards Sohan Lal, who was manifestly unsuccessful and unconfident. He knew his father would have urged him towards Mr Chaddha; and while not exactly turning him away from Sohan Lal, would nevertheless have brought it to his notice that there was really not much of a good example to be got from poor Sohan Lal, who found it hard to keep discipline among his students and was repressed and melancholy through the effort of supporting a large family on a small income.

In his disappointment with himself, it again occurred to Prem that he really ought to make a second attempt on Mr Khanna for the rise in salary. The first attempt had to be regarded in the light merely of groundwork, on which he must now start building an edifice of persuasion. But these things, he told himself, had above all to be done with subtlety and tact; and what occasion better for subtlety and tact than a tea-party? Anything could happen at a tea-party: meeting him thus, for the first time on social terms, Mr Khanna might take a great liking to him; or perhaps Indu, if she behaved nicely, might make a good impression and dispose Mr Khanna to regard them as a deserving young couple who should be given all help and encouragement in their struggle with life. So he decided to postpone his second attempt on the Principal till after Sunday's tea-party had given him opportunity to improve his position.

But his first attempt on his landlord was still open. He disliked the prospect of asking Mr Seigal for a reduction in rent, and half realized that dislike had been quietly prompting him to indefinite postponements. But it was such postponements, he now told himself, which were responsible for his position of unsuccess. 'Strive and strive and strive again!' he exhorted himself, with a show of bravery; and turned promptly to the wrong person for advice and encouragement.

'Mr Sohan Lal,' he said, 'do you think it is possible to ask a landlord to take less rent?'

The bell rang, indicating the end of their little break. Mr Chaddha shut his book smartly and got up at once to go to his class-room. Prem felt constrained to follow him. He was always afraid of arriving in the class-room later than Mr Chaddha, for he knew his students would be noisy and perhaps disturb Mr Chaddha. Sohan Lal too got up to go to his class-room; but, like Prem, he did so if not reluctantly then at least with a certain melancholy resignation.

'A landlord must understand that a man's burdens increase as he becomes older,' Prem said, out in the narrow little corridor.

'They increase,' agreed Sohan Lal with a gentle sigh. They were standing outside his class-room. His students were having a pretence game of volley ball. They were tossing a rubber from one to another, shouting 'Pass this side!' and taking up attitudes of mock defence. Sohan Lal glanced in apprehensively.

'A landlord must have feeling. When a person is in difficulties, he cannot only say to him go away.'

'It would be wrong,' Sohan Lal agreed.

'On the contrary, he must help that person and be like a father to him. We must all have love and help one another.'

'Here, this side!' came lusty voices out of Sohan Lal's class-room, and there was a noise of pushing and laughing, of hard young bodies in energetic action. From farther down the corridor came Mr Chaddha's voice raised in lecture tone. Reluctantly – for he found his present discussion very interesting – Prem started towards his class-room. He could hear Sohan Lal ineffectively calling to his students: 'Please be in your seats!'

On the way home he reverted to thoughts about how people ought to help one another and love one another. 'What am I by myself?' he thought. 'I can do nothing, I am weak and helpless and need the support of a father.' He wanted to go to Mr Seigal and say to him, 'You are my father', and stand before him, humble and submissive, like a child. Then Mr Seigal would see that it was his duty to reduce the rent.

When he reached the house, he at once knocked on the Seigals' door before he could weaken in his resolution. Through the fly-screen he could see the Seigals' son Romesh sitting on the sofa, reading a film magazine. Romesh called 'Come in' and seemed pleased to see Prem. He showed his magazine and said, 'I am very fond of the cinema. I go three times a week, and sometimes four.'

Romesh Seigal was very much like Prem's students – healthy, cheerful, wearing good clothes and an expensive wristwatch. So Prem found himself addressing him in the same way as he addressed his students; he said 'And your studies?' in a somewhat stern voice.

'I am not too fond of studies,' Romesh said frankly.

'You must study hard,' Prem said, 'and pass in your examinations. Then perhaps you will be able to secure a good position with the Government and your parents will be pleased.'

'I find studies very boring,' Romesh said, 'I like only pictures very much.'

'What will you learn from going to pictures? This is only amusement for an idle hour. While you are a student, you must learn and strive to pass in your examinations and do not think of amusement at all.'

'Quite right,' said Mr Seigal, emerging from the next room. Prem got up and greeted him with hands deferentially joined. Though it was past six o'clock in the evening, Mr Seigal seemed to have only just got up from his afternoon sleep. His hair and his shirt were rumpled and wet with perspiration, and he was yawning so widely that tears came into his eyes.

'This is what I am always telling him,' said Mr Seigal when he had finished yawning.

'We were having a little chat,' said Prem, feeling rather sheepish.

'Please take trouble with him,' said Mr Seigal. 'You are a teacher, a lecturer in a college, he can learn only what is good from you.'

Though at any other time Prem might have felt flattered by these observations, now he found them rather awkward. He wanted Mr Seigal to look on him as another son, as helpless and dependent as his own son Romesh, and here he was being set up as a mentor to that son. He shuffled his feet and smiled deprecatingly. He wanted to look young and foolish, yet somehow, after what Mr Seigal had said, he could not help feeling elderly and responsible; and so when he spoke he spoke in that role, as one weighed down by years and re-sponsibilities. 'It is our duty,' he said, 'to guide young men and set them on the right path in Life.'

Mr Seigal grunted as he picked up a newspaper, yawned some more and rubbed his hand over his hair. Romesh had gone back to reading his film magazine, humming a melancholy love song as he did so.

'In our ancient writings it is written,' Prem continued, 'that there are four stages to a man's life. When he is young, he is a student, learning from his father and his teachers – '

'Has the tea been brought?' Mr Seigal inquired of Romesh.

'After that comes the life of the householder,' Prem said. 'In this stage a man must raise a family and see to their needs . . .' He thought of Indu and the coming baby and felt instantly depressed. At this point he would like to have joined his hands in supplication and asked for a reduction in rent. But he felt shy, especially before Romesh whom he was to serve as a good example, so he continued. 'The third stage is when a man retires from his duties as a householder and spends his time in contemplation.'

'They have made vegetables samusas with our tea,' Romesh told his father.

'Thus it may be clearly seen,' Prem concluded miserably, skipping the fourth stage, of which he was not quite sure, 'that each stage of life has its own duties and obligations.' Oppressed by a sense of failure, he took his leave rather quickly. Upstairs Indu was sitting knitting pink bootees. He said to her at once, 'There are some things in which a wife can be very helpful to her husband.' Indu moved her lips silently, counting her stitches; she seemed in deep concentration. 'A wife must share her husband's burden!' Prem suddenly shouted.

Indu quickly wound up her knitting and put it away in a paper bag. Even though he was angry, Prem noticed how deft and neat she was in her ways.

'It is you who should speak to the Seigals,' he said.

Silently she handed him a letter. He saw that it was from his mother, but did not open it for a while. 'For you it would be easy. All you would have to do – '

'My mother writes my uncle will come and fetch me home next time he is in Delhi on business.'

'What?'

'My mother writes – '

'I told you you cannot go. My mother is coming to visit us. This letter probably . . .' He opened it and when he had read it, looked rather smug. 'Yes, she is coming next week.'

Indu abruptly left the room. Prem read his mother's letter again. He was very happy that she was coming; and of course it was out of the question that Indu should go away. He followed her into the kitchen to tell her so, but found only the servant-boy there. The boy was washing dishes and making a lot of clatter as he did so; he looked up at Prem as if challenging him to dare say something. As a matter of fact, Prem would have liked to say something, to assert his authority in the home, but meeting the boy's bold gaze, he contented himself with only making an important face and then retreated. He found Indu in the bedroom lying on the bed, turned over on her side and with her eyes shut. He was sure she was not asleep, but did not know how to disprove it. He sat down on the other end of the bed, hoping she would get tired of pretending. There were quite a number of things he wanted to talk to her about – about her not being able to go home and the rent and Mr Khanna's tea-party.

Furtively he looked at her back which was turned towards him. Her hip rose in a fine curve and the sari was clinging to her in such a way that the shape of one buttock and tapering thigh were clearly outlined. Prem swallowed, and looked away. He looked at the opposite wall and noted how badly it had been whitewashed. It was hot in the room and intermingled with the heat was the smell of her perspiration and her hair-oil. He thought it would be better to go away, but his limbs felt heavy and reluctant, and it was only with some effort that he got himself out of the room. He felt his heart beating loudly and this continued even after he had left the house and was walking in the streets. He walked for a long time and all the time his thoughts were unworthy and filled him with shame, but he could not stop thinking them.

Wednesday evening was a great occasion for him. He left the college in a hurry, went home and dressed himself very smartly in a clean shirt and his best trousers; he also put a lot of hair-oil on his hair so that it became one smooth shining mass. He took good care that Indu should see him when he was ready and walked up and down several times in front of her where she was sitting on a mat in the sitting-room with her knitting. But though he cleared his throat, wound his watch and smoothed his hair, she apparently did not notice; nor did she ask him where he was going, which was disappointing for he would like to have told her how he was going by invitation to take tea with a German boy.

The address Hans had given him was an impressive one in the best part of New Delhi. The road was wide and shaded by rows of well-grown trees. The houses were very beautiful, all white with pillared fronts and large green lawns and flowers growing in painted pots. Hans' house was not so beautiful. It was equally large and the veranda had pillars, but it was cracked and crumbling in brown patches and the garden in front was dry and tangled. Prem walked up the driveway and into the veranda. One of the french windows was open, so he went in and found himself in a room with an old carpet, three faded red plush armchairs and a lot of dusty books. Someone was sitting in one of the armchairs reading a book which was held so high that the face was quite covered by it. Emerging from the top of the armchair was a tousle of blonde-grey hair and from its bottom a pair of stout white legs. The book was lowered and a lady's face emerged square and red. The lady smiled, pushing her stout cheeks upwards, and said in a voice which was deep like a man's and yet, in its intonation, seductive to the point of exaggeration: 'Hallo ... Looking for *me?*'

Prem clenched his fists by his side and he said, much louder and shriller than he had intended, 'Hans Loewe!' and it sounded not so much a request as a cry for help.

'Oh, you're Hans' friend, are you?' said the lady in the same gruff honeyed voice.

'He asked me for tea.'

'Asked you for tea, did he?'

'At six o' clock.'

'Did he now? Well, we'll have to do something about it then, won't we? What's your name?' When he had told her, she said, 'Sit down, Prem dear. Talk to me.'

'Perhaps he has forgotten . . . I will come another day.'

'Oh, he's home all right, dear. Doing his exercises, I expect. I know the armchairs don't look very clean and you've put on such a nice pair of trousers, haven't you, but you'll really have to sit down if you don't want to hurt my feelings.' Prem said down instantly.

'Yogic exercises, you know. He's getting quite good at them. What do you do?'

'I am a lecturer at – '

'No, dear. Which Yoga do you do? Hatha Yoga or Bhakti Yoga or what?'

'I don't think I – '

'Well you should. We all should. How do you think you'll meet the Eternal and the Infinite if you don't? I'm Hans's landlady. Everybody calls me Kitty.' The room smelt of dust deep-ingrained; the skylight windows set under the ceiling were smeared and opaque, and lurking high in corners were shreds of cobwebs. A very old and shaky fan creaked noisily from the ceiling.

'If he is busy, I will come again,' Prem said, not however daring to rise.

'I've got a room free just now, if you're interested.'

'What a marvellous idea!' cried Hans who entered just then. 'Come and live with us, Prem!'

'And be our love,' said the landlady. She chuckled: 'That's a quotation, you know, Come and live with me and be my love, and we will all the something something.'

'English poetry is so rich,' Hans said politely. 'It is the room next to mine, Prem. We will talk all day and share our thoughts and in the nights we will talk more and drink black coffee to keep us awake. What friends we will be with each other!'

Prem sat on the edge of a frayed armchair. He held himself stiff and his hands were pushed between his knees. He wanted to be polite and sociable but felt very shy.

Kitty heaved herself to her feet. When she stood up, she was big and square and dressed in a belted black cotton dress with white dots on it which left a lot of heavy white arm and leg exposed. She said, 'Let's see if that Mohammed Ali will come across with any tea for us – seeing as we have a guest.'

'Since we met I have had a marvellous adventure,' Hans said. He was sitting, not on one of the armchairs though there were three of them in the room, but on the floor with his legs crossed under him. He was wearing shorts and a pale blue Aertex shirt with tiny cap sleeves. His legs and feet were large and naked and white like chicken-flesh. 'Something has woken in me. You are surprised?' Prem nodded though he hardly knew what Hans was saying. He could hear Kitty shouting, 'Hey, Mohammed Ali!' and her voice echoing as through a large and empty house. 'Yes, I also was surprised,' Hans said. 'I thought to my-self. Already? But it is true. I feel so humble,' he said, folding his hands and laying his head wistfully to one side. 'I ask myself, can I be worthy?'

Kitty came back and said, 'The trouble with Mohammed Ali is he *despises* me so.'

'Can I be worthy?' Hans repeated.

'Everybody's worthy,' Kitty said. 'But I don't think you've really come to anything yet.'

'Yes, yes, it was real!' Hans cried. 'I felt it, God-consciousness, I felt Him moving here, here, at the base of my spine!' He hit that place hard with his fist and cried: 'What joy it was for me! I wanted to cry like a little child cries when it sees its mother. Mother, I wanted to shout, Mammi!'

'It's hard to tell with these things, especially with an excitable person like you.'

'It is true that I am high-strung,' Hans said with an air of modesty.

'What about you?' Kitty said, turning abruptly to Prem who smiled and pushed his hands farther between his knees.

'I think he is very advanced,' Hans said. 'He looks so spiritual.'

'They all look spiritual,' Kitty said gloomily. 'Even this fellow,' she added, as the bearer came in carrying a tea-tray. He wore what once must have been a fine uniform but which now had turned grey, had only the faintest traces of red braiding and tufts of cotton where gold buttons had been. He was unshaven and visibly dirty, and his face

44

bore an expression of profound melancholy. 'All right, Mohammed Ali, that'll be all, thank you,' Kitty told him when he had softly placed the tray before her. 'You see,' she said, 'once I thought he despised me because of this deep spiritual quality which I thought he had and I hadn't.'

'The man's eyes!' Hans cried. 'All Eternity is there seen like in a mirror!'

'Yes, well, that's what I used to think,' Kitty said. 'Now I'm not so sure. Oh drat it, the milk's sour again.'

'Oh drat,' Hans echoed, looking sad.

'It's because I'm not like the British sahibs and mem-sahibs of old that he despises me so. He misses it all so much, poor dear – the hordes of servants and the dinner-parties and Simla in the summer and all that.'

'You are too materialistic,' Hans said.

'Not me, him,' Kitty said.

'He does not think of such things at all. He has withdrawn himself from the world and contemplates. How sour your tea is always, bah, this is terrible to drink.'

'You want to come to a party with me, dear?' Kitty, asked Prem.

'He is my guest,' Hans pointed out.

'Well next Saturday he can be my guest. I'll take him to Peggy's party.'

'We must talk!' Hans cried, thumping his fist on Prem's knee. 'Everything must be shared between friends, all thoughts and wishes and adventures, if they are of the body or the spirit!' Though this was consonant with Prem's own opinions about friendship, he felt too shy and too bewildered to respond. 'Without a friend,' Hans said, 'to whom I can lay bare my soul, I cannot live.'

'Goodness,' said Kitty in calm surprise.

Hans put both his hands on Prem's shoulders and his pale blue eyes behind the rimless spectacles scanned Prem's face. 'Now I must have the truth from you,' he said sternly.

'Of course,' Prem murmured. To avoid Han's searching glance, he slid his own eyes sideways to look appealingly at Kitty, who however was paying no attention. She was bending over the tea-tray, with her big bottom in its black and white cotton dress stuck out at one end and her head at the other; her lips were moving slightly and she looked preoccupied and even a little sinister as she poured all the tea left over in the cups back into teapot.

'You are my friend,' Hans said. 'You must tell me the truth.' His hands lay heavy on Prem's shoulders. 'Do you think a Westerner like me can reach to the spiritual greatness of the Indian yogis?'

Prem said, 'Everything is possible if one tries.'

Hans took away his hands and cried in agony, 'But I have tried – oh, my God, how have I tried!' In his agitation he took a few skips round the room on his naked feet, raising them high up so that it looked as if he had stepped on a nail and hurt himself.

'Well that's something, isn't it,' Kitty said.

'In here I have a great longing to feel, to *be*! You, Prem, are Indian, you understand what is this longing that has come to me – '

'You can pick us up Saturday evening for Peggy's party,' Kitty told Prem.

Hans said, 'Please tell the washerman to bring back my good shirt for this day.' He put his arm round Prem's shoulder and walked him out on to the veranda. 'So, my friend,' he said, 'we have had a good conversation.' Mohammed Ali was squatting on the top step of the veranda, enjoying a little brown cigarette which he held cupped in his hand. He looked up at them sourly, but made no move to rise.

When Prem got home, lights were burning in all the rooms of the Seigals' house and there were visitors and card-playing on the veranda. But upstairs in his own house all was darkness and silence. Indu was lying on the bed fast asleep. The kitchen was empty, though there was still a spark of fire in the grate. Perched on top of the pile of ashes was a pot and on the lid of the pot lay a few dry chapattis. This, he supposed, was his food. He was hungry, so he sat down on the floor of the kitchen and ate. But he knew it was not right for a wife to go to sleep before she had served her husband however late he might come. He considered for a moment whether to wake her up and tell her so. But he did not feel angry enough for that. He was still a little dazed from his visit and kept thinking about Hans and Kitty. Their interest in spiritual matters puzzled him, for he had always thought that Europeans were very materialistic in their outlook.

The servant-boy appeared and Prem at once began to scold him for going out. As usual, the boy took no notice of him, except to assume a somewhat contemptuous expression. 'Until the master of the house has taken his food,' Prem told him, 'your place is in the kitchen.' 'Finished?' the boy asked and took away Prem's empty pot for cleaning.

Prem lay down next to Indu on the bed. He could hear her regular breathing and at once forgot about Hans and Kitty and about everything else. He sat up and looked at her. There was a very dim light in the room, which came from a street-lamp a few houses farther down. He could just make out her shape as she lay there. He had already begun to notice that she had changed, that her hips and breasts, always fine and plump and round, had become burgeoning and luxurious. He supposed it was the baby. Reverently he placed his hand on her stomach and thought about how it was his child in there. But not for long. Soon his hand had found the string at her waist to untie her petticoat. After a while she woke up. She turned her head away to hide her face, but did not try to hide anything else.

Next morning, though, Prem was in a stern mood with her again. He watched her drinking her tea and noticed regretfully that she was not doing so with the refinement which would be required at Mr Khanna's tea-party. He brooded about this for a while, then got up and followed her into the bedroom. She was lovingly dusting a picture of Mother and Baby which she had recently acquired and hung up on the bedroom wall. Baby was very stout, with big folds in its legs, and Mother had a simpering expression and held a sunflower in one hand.

'When you drink tea,' Prem said, 'you must hold your little finger up in the air, like this.' He demonstrated, and she watched him in amazement. Suddenly she gave a very strange sound and continued quickly with her dusting. 'What is there to laugh at?' he said crossly.

'Mind yourself!' cried the servant-boy, lustily swinging a wet floorcloth around Prem's feet. Prem stepped back hastily; from outside the door he complained: 'He is completely without respect.'

'He has to clean the room,' Indu said.

'In my father's house, the servant never dared to enter the room when my father was there. And when he spoke to my father, he joined his hands and said "Your Honour". Come out here, I must speak with you.' But when she came, he did not know what he wanted to say. She stood before him, patiently waiting, with the duster still in her hand. 'So tell me,' he said and cleared his throat and looked important while trying to think what he should tell him. 'Yes,' he said, 'tell me – you have heard from your mother again?'

'She says when my uncle is in Delhi on business next time –'

'This you have already told me. And I have told you that of course it is impossible for you to go away with your uncle.'

She went back to her dusting without a word.

'Because my mother is coming to see us!' he called after her into the room. She gave no indication of having heard him, and the servant-boy swished his cloth in wide sweeps.

Prem left the house in a stern and rather assertive mood, and this was still with him by the time he reached the college. There were as usual many students clustered outside in the street; they stood together in groups or leant against the walls with their hands in their pockets and a bored and cynical expression on their faces. A girl was passing on the other side of the road. She was a short and stocky Punjabi peasant, not at all pretty, but the boys were bored enough to aim some desultory whistles at her. Prem, in his stern mood, felt instantly outraged. He swung round at one group of boys and demanded 'Why did you whistle?' He was not at all sure that it was they who had whistled, but he had to confront someone. 'Have you no shame,' he said, 'to behave in this indecent manner?'

Other students pressed closer to listen. The accused boys began to protest that it was not they who had whistled, but Prem would not listen to them. 'What sort of behaviour is that,' he said, 'to injure and insult innocent young girls?' He thought of Indu. If she passed, they would whistle at her.

'Come with me instantly to the Principal!' he shouted. 'I will see to it that the sternest disciplinary action is taken against you.'

Still protesting their innocence, the boys accompanied him upstairs to Mr Khanna's living quarters. Mr Khanna was sitting in an arm-chair with his feet up, reading the paper. He did not look at all pleased to see them.

Prem was too angry to feel his usual shyness before the Principal. He burst out at once, 'Sir, these boys were behaving in an indecent manner in the street.'

Mr Khanna shut his eyes in weary resignation and laid aside his newspaper.

'They were insulting a girl with whistles,' Prem said.

Mr Khanna turned to the boys and said, 'This is a very grave charge.'

'It is abominable behaviour!' Prem cried.

'What have you to say for yourselves?' Mr Khanna asked the boys, but before they could reply, Prem cried: 'I demand the severest punishment for them!'

'Sir,' said the boys, 'we did not do it.'

'Go to your class-rooms,' Mr Khanna said. 'I will deal with you later.' Prem glared at them furiously as they trooped out of the room. 'It is boys like these,' he told the Principal, 'who ruin the good name of our college.'

'You are sure it was they who whistled?'

'Quite sure, sir,' Prem replied with confidence. He really was quite sure now. Anger had swept aside all hesitation.

'And they whistled only? Nothing else?'

'A disgrace to the college! An example must be made of them!'

'I am glad you reported the matter to me,' Mr Khanna said, taking up his newspaper again and trying to locate the paragraph he had been reading.

'It was my duty to do so, sir. We have wives, sisters, daughters – how can we protect their honour if we fail to uproot evil and shamelessness from among us?' He felt virtuous and grown up. He was a family man, upholding the sanctity of the family against the assaults of immorality. For a moment it struck him that here was an opportunity to appeal for a rise in salary. He could point out to Mr Khanna that a man with a family to support and protect, such as he was, needed more than 175 rupees a month on which to do so. But he felt it would not be consonant with his present high moral stand to introduce any personal note. 'It pains me to see that there are such elements in the college,' he said, assuming a pained expression.

A bell rang downstairs in the college. Mr Khanna lowered his paper and said with a pleased look on his face, 'I think there is the bell for your lesson.'

Prem was satisfied with himself for the rest of the morning. He felt he had acted like a responsible teacher, with moral fervour and stern solicitude for those in his charge. His father himself, he thought, could not have behaved better. During their breaktime he gave a lecture on discipline to Sohan Lal. 'We must be like severe though loving fathers to our students,' he told him. Mr Chaddha, overhearing Prem's remark, took interest and pleasure in the subject and contributed a few forceful opinions of his own to which Prem listened with his head held to one side and nodding it from time to time in pleased agreement. Sohan Lal seemed rather embarrassed, but neither Mr Chaddha nor Prem took any notice of him.

So when Prem went home for his lunch, he was in a sterner mood than ever. He saw no reason why, now that he was a success as a teacher, he should not be a success as a husband too. He would have been quite pleased if his food had been slightly delayed, but Indu was very prompt with it. He cleared his throat and looked authoritative as he sat down on the floor in front of his brass tray. She kept bringing him more hot chapattis. Everything was going very nicely and he enjoyed his meal. Maybe he was a successful husband already. Even her cooking, it seemed to him, had improved – or was it just that he was getting used to it? When he had finished, he asked her to prepare a betel-leaf. She was very good, he had to admit at preparing betel-leaves.

But when he went into the bedroom, he saw that she had taken out her suitcase. It was lying on the bed with the lid open. He called her and pointed at it: 'What is this?' he demanded.

She whipped it quickly off the bed and shut it. 'I have put it out for airing,' she said.

'You are intending to go on a journey?'

'Only if my uncle comes . . .'

Prem swallowed hard. He felt it to be right that he should be angry, but he wanted it to be a controlled anger. So he said in a quiet though forceful voice, 'I have forbidden you.'

But suddenly it was Indu who was angry and her anger was not at all controlled. 'Who are you to forbid?' she shouted.

This took him aback considerably. The answer to her question seemed to him so very obvious that he could not understand how she came to ask it. But before he could point that out to her, she was shouting some more. 'Now we have come to the limit! Now he forbids!' She gave a sound of contempt. 'He forbids me!' she snorted and stamped her foot. The servant-boy came running from the kitchen and stared at her. 'Now we have come to this!' Indu shouted.

Prem was very much embarrassed. He glanced at the servant-boy and told Indu in a low voice, 'Please speak more quietly.' Quite apart from the servant-boy, there were also the Seigals – supposing they heard, what would they think?

Indu turned to the servant-boy and shouted at him, 'Who called you here?' The boy ran back to the kitchen and immediately began to make a loud and busy noise with pots.

'Please speak more quietly,' Prem urged her again. 'We can sit down and discuss quietly.' He put out his hand as if to pull her down to sit on the bed, but she jumped a step backwards crying, 'Leave me alone! Don't touch me!' Then she ran and locked herself in the bathroom.

Prem stood there helpless for a while. He did not know what to do and could only wait for her to come out again. When she did not come, he went and knocked very softly on the door. There was no sound from inside. He put his mouth to the door-frame and said in a low voice, 'Please come out.' He waited, but there was still no response. 'We can discuss together,' he murmured through the door. Inside there was no movement at all, but he heard a slight noise behind him. He turned and found the servant-boy standing there looking at him, so he quickly moved away from the door and pretended to be talking to himself.

Indu gave no indication of wanting to come out, and it was time for him to go back to his afternoon lessons. He did not like to leave the situation like this, but he had to go. Slowly he went down the stairs; slowly and thoughtfully he walked along the road. He was feeling depressed and very unsure of himself. Perhaps she is right, he thought; who am I to forbid? All his confident thoughts about himself as husband and teacher had gone.

The road was so hot and still. Even the little shopman, who sold cigarettes, betel-leaves and cold drinks, sat sleeping in his hut of a shop. Prem as he passed looked longingly at the red ice-box in which the cold drinks were stored. The afternoon heat was making him feel very thirsty. But he was at once ashamed of his longing: like a child, he thought, I crave for sweets. If one wishes to control others, one must first learn to control one's own senses; and he thought about how bad he was at controlling his own senses. How often, for instance, he thought indecent thoughts about Indu, when he saw her lying next to him or moving about the house, and wanted to do things with her which should be reserved only for the dark and the night. And before his marriage, he had not only thought but even talked, with Raj and other friends, about girls and what it might be like to sleep with them. So what sort of a teacher, what sort of an authority, could be set himself up to be? Who was he to censor boys for doing no more than whistle at a passing girl?

And perhaps it had not even been those boys. Now that he had grown unsure of himself again he felt unsure of that too. Yet he had asked Mr Khanna to take the sternest disciplinary action against them. Maybe Mr Khanna was going to expel them. Maybe he was going to expel these boys who might be innocent. When he got to the college, Prem did not hesitate. He walked straight up to the first floor and entered Mr Khanna's living-room. 'I must speak with you very urgently, please, sir,' he said in agitation.

Mr and Mrs Khanna were having their midday meal. They ate in English style, sitting facing one another at a table and using fork and spoon. Mrs Khanna had just speared a piece of cauliflower pickle on to the point of her fork and she was holding it like a trident while she looked furiously at Prem.

'It is very urgent, sir,' Prem said. He felt greatly embarrassed and would like to have gone away; but he had to talk to Mr Khanna straightaway, before it was too late and the boys already expelled.

'It is disgraceful,' said Mrs Khanna, depositing the pickle on the side of her plate, 'that the Principal of this college cannot have private time even when he eats his meal.'

'It is about those boys,' Prem said miserably.

Mr Khanna's head was bent close over his plate and he was engaged in shovelling a great amount of food into his mouth.

'Perhaps I made a mistake,' Prem confessed.

'Certainly you made a mistake!' cried Mrs Khanna. 'Is this a time to come?'

'Perhaps it was other boys who whistled,' Prem said. He joined his hands in supplication and said, 'Please pardon them, sir.'

Mr Khanna went on eating without looking up from his plate.

'They are young,' said Prem. 'What do they know what is right and what is wrong? We must be lenient with them, sir.'

'What pleasure can there be in food if it is not eaten in peace?' Mrs Khanna demanded.

'And perhaps it was not those boys at all!' Prem gently moaned, wringing his hands.

Mr Khanna pulled his napkin out of the waistband of his trousers and wiped his mouth with it. 'One must be very careful in bringing accusation,' he told Prem.

'I know it, sir,' said Prem, humbly.

'You have finished already?' cried Mrs Khanna, as her husband laid aside his crumpled napkin.

'To punish the innocent in place of the guilty is a heinous crime,' Mr Khanna said.

Prem nodded his head which was sunk right down on to his chest in shame.

'What is the use of my cooking, cooking, cooking,' Mrs Khanna demanded, 'if you don't eat properly?'

'The meat was not soft,' Mr Khanna said. 'The teacher must be stern as a judge but also just as a judge.'

'I know it, sir,' Prem whispered.

Mrs Khanna cried: 'Your pleasure in your food is destroyed by interruption, and then it is my fault!'

'Just as a judge also,' Mr Khanna repeated emphatically to Prem.

Afterwards Prem felt slightly better. He had confessed his mistake and so averted any evil consequences it might have had. But he was still sad. He felt himself to be terribly inadequate as a husband, a teacher, as an adult altogether. After classes he waited for Sohan Lal and told him so. Sohan Lal was tying his tiffin-carrier to his bicycle; he did not make any reply to Prem's confession, but said instead, 'Today I am not going home.'

Prem said, 'I thought once one is married and is earning money, one will become different.'

'Perhaps you will like to come with me?' Sohan Lal suggested.

Prem did not ask where to, but he reflected for a moment. Really he ought to go home and see that Indu had let herself out of the bathroom and perhaps pacify her a little. But supposing she was still angry, and would shout at him again, within earshot of the servant-boy and the Seigals? 'Thank you,' he told Sohan Lal, 'I will like to come.'

When they had got far enough from the college they both sat on the bicycle. Prem was on the saddle and Sohan Lal sat sideways on the bar and gave directions. When they had to turn right or left, Sohan Lal held out an arm. The tiffin-carrier clattered from the handlebar. There was no bell, but when necessary, Sohan Lal shouted 'Look out!' Prem pedalled with pleasure, and a breeze ran through his hair.

They cycled a long way, right into the heart of the old city. Here in a narrow lane running off the main bazaar, Sohan Lal stopped them. In this lane there were mostly large prosperous cloth-shops, with large prosperous merchants sitting crosslegged inside them, smoking hookahs or chewing betel-leaves and looking more like gentlemen of leisure taking their ease than like shopkeepers anxious to sell. Sohan Lal led Prem into an arched gateway set slightly back between two shops, then through another arch leading off that one. Now they were in a paved courtyard. Under a tree sat a cobbler slowly hammering at a heel. A horse was being led out of the gateway and a cook went running into a door with a dead chicken held by its neck.

Sohan Lal carefully locked up his cycle and then he led Prem into a little doorway and up a dark and narrow winding stair. They went right up to the top of the house, till they came to a curved wooden door which was so low that they had to stoop to pass through it. Now they were in a room with, so it seemed to Prem, a great many people in it. They sat on the floor, with their hands clasped round their knees; they were all of them smiling and their eyes were fixed on a bearded swami in an orange robe who sat crosslegged on a string-bed with his beads held loosely in his hand. The swami was also smiling, and he looked altogether very happy. Sohan Lal at once went up to him and touched his feet with respect. The swami affectionately tousled Sohan Lal's hair and said, 'You have been neglecting me.'

Sohan Lal said, 'If only I could, I would like to be with you all day and all night.'

'This is exactly how the lover speaks to the girl he has been neglecting,' the swami said. Everybody laughed, including Sohan Lal and the swami. Someone said, 'We are all your lovers', and the swami replied 'And you all neglect me', which brought more laughter. 'It is like this, you see,' said the swami. 'Sometimes you love me very much and then you come running to me; but at other times you think – oh my wife, oh my job, oh my little finger which is hurting me, and then you don't remember me at all. Isn't that true?' he asked Sohan Lal who looked sad and replied, 'You must forgive us.'

The swami smiled very sweetly and chucked Sohan Lal under the chin, so that he did not look sad any more. 'Today I see you have brought me a new visitor,' said the swami. Prem came forward, and he too touched the swami's feet. 'Oh-ho,' said the swami, 'so good to me already.'

'He is my colleague,' Sohan Lal said. Prem was aware of everyone looking at him, but he did not feel particularly shy. There did not seem to be any cause for shyness in such good-humoured company.

'It is nice of you to come,' the swami told him. 'But you must be feeling hot. Please give him some water,' he said to one of the young men sitting near him.

Prem said he was not thirsty. Someone said. 'Seeing you, he feels refreshed.'

'I would like to refresh him, if he will let me,' said the swami looking at Prem with what seemed to be love.

'Chant the name of God to him then,' someone said.

'What is the use of my chanting if his ears are stopped with wax?' the swami replied.

'Wash them for him,' they suggested.

'This is exactly what I would like to do,' the swami said. He motioned Prem and Sohan Lal to sit on the floor with the others. 'I would like to wash everyone's ears,' he said. 'But most people won't let me.'

Someone said, 'The trouble is that most of us don't know what is valuable in the world and what is worthless.'

'We all run after trash,' said someone else.

'Once a prince passed with his attendants through a poor village,' the swami said. 'The prince dropped a diamond ring there but he was in a hurry and did not even notice its loss. One of his menials had a worthless glass bauble, which broke, so that he had no further use for it and he threw it away. The villagers fought bitterly about this broken glass bauble. But the prince's diamond ring they did not even bother to pick up, for it seemed a thing of no value to them.'

Some more people came in, and one of them said, 'You are telling stories again?'

'To amuse my friends,' the swami said, 'to make them love me and want to come to see me often.'

'All day we run after broken glass baubles,' someone said. 'It is only you who teach us to pick up the prince's diamond ring.'

Prem looked round the room and saw that most of the people there were young men. Some of them wore beautifully starched clothes of fine white muslin; others looked shabby and poor. There were also a few older men, and some of these too wore good clothes and looked like successful doctors or lawyers, while others, like Sohan Lal, were careworn and threadbare and obviously not in the least successful. But all of them now had an eager bright air about them, as they sat there on the floor looking up at the swami perched on his bed. Prem too looked up at the swami and, like the others, he could not take his eyes away again.

A very fat man entered, wearing a dhoti and a thin muslin shirt over it. Behind him came servants carrying baskets of sweetmeats and flower garlands, which the fat man placed at the swami's feet. 'Ah,' said the swami, 'Sethji is treating us again today.'

A young man said, 'Do you think you ought to accept things from Sethji?'

'I am happy that he thinks of me,' the swami said.

'But he is so tainted with worldly interest,' said the younger man.

'I am not sure we ought to allow him to come near you at all,' said another.

'Now keep quiet,' said Sethji, who was busy untying the string from the baskets he had brought. When he had done so, he offered the sweetmeats to the swami who broke off a piece and tasted it and then sent the rest round the room. Everyone ate; they were very good sweatmeats. Someone said, 'If he brings sweetmeats like this, perhaps we will allow him to come after all.'

'You are a pack of rogues,' said Sethji.

The swami laughed and said, 'They are all my beloved rogues.' The flower garlands lay at his feet, pervading the room with a strong sweet smell.

'Rogues we may be,' said one young man. 'But we come here to talk of God.'

'What do you know of these things?' mocked Sethji.

The swami said, 'Only as the child knows its mother, so we know God. When the child goes out into the street to play with its companions, then it becomes so engrossed in its game that it forgets the mother at home.'

Someone said, 'So when Sethji goes out to make money – '

'And that he does all the time,' someone else gaily called between.

' – then he forgets all about God.'

'But when the child falls down and hurts itself,' said the swami, 'it again remembers its mother and goes running to her, crying for comfort.'

'Which means,' said a young man, 'when the Income Tax comes after Sethji, then he goes crying to God.'

Everyone laughed, even Sethji, and the swami said, 'You are in a very naughty mood today.' Prem looked at him and looked. He had never seen anyone like the swami. His face was like a child's, so laughing and clear and happy; there was a glow in his cheeks and his eyes shone.

A young man started to sing. He sat there on the floor, with his legs tucked under him, a young man with close-shaved hair and a badly sewn striped shirt. 'What is this longing I have for you?' he sang. 'God, let me come to you.' His voice was low and sweet and appealing, like a lover's. The swami's eyes, as he listened, misted over with longing and his lips were parted in an expression which was part joy and part anguish.

When the young man had finished singing there was a murmur of approval all round the room. The swami said, 'When I hear singing like that, I don't know how it is with me – ' His voice broke and Prem

56

noticed with surprise that tears came rushing out from his eyes. 'Oh,
Ram Ram Ram!' the swami called, and then he laughed, while the
tears were still flowing down his cheeks and he took up the flower
garlands and flung them towards a group of young men. 'Oh, God,' he
sang, 'let me adore your feet!' and he sang with such ecstasy and
fervour that everyone was moved, and some wept and some laughed,
and then some more people were singing and one young man draped
the garlands round his neck and danced. Prem was laughing with joy,
though at the same time there were tears in his eyes, and he clapped
his hands in time with the singing and shouted 'Wah!' in delight.

Late at night he went home. He did not want to go, especially when
he saw that several of the others, including Sohan Lal, were intending
to stay the night. Prem too wanted to stay with the swami and his
followers; he wanted to be one of them, eat with them, sleep with
them, pray with them, be with them always. But Sohan Lal told him
he had better go home or his wife would be worried. 'Next time,
perhaps,' Sohan Lal said, 'you will stay.' The swami asked him, 'You
will come to see me again?' Prem touched his feet very reverently and
replied, in a voice shaking with emotion, 'I will come always, every
day I will come.'

The swami laughed and shook his finger at him. 'Now you are
talking with too much extravagance.'

'It is true,' Prem said. 'Really – I promise.'

'If you want to come,' said the swami, 'then come. But only because
you want to, not because you have promised.'

'I will always want to,' Prem said with sincerity and fervour.

Later he could not remember how he got home. He felt light-
headed, and kept laughing to himself. Probably people who met him
thought he was drunk. In a way that was how he felt. But it was not so
much as if he had drunk spirits than as if he had drunk pure well-
water, and it was the unaccustomed purity of it that had gone to his
head. He lay at home in bed, with Indu fast asleep beside him, and felt
as if he were floating, he was so light and clear and happy. He thought
yes, this is how one must live – with love and laughter and song and
thoughts of God. All his former worries about his rent, his rise in
salary, his lack of authority as teacher and husband, were nothing but
a thin scum floating on top of a deep well of happiness and satisfaction. Nothing, he thought, would ever trouble him again. From now
on he would live in contemplation only of spiritual things. Indu would

be like a sister to him – he would love her as a sister and both would sit at the feet of the swami and think of God and indulge in happy, innocent play.

He wanted to tell her so, and he leant towards her gently to shake her shoulder. She went on sleeping. One cheek was pressed deep into her pillow and she was breathing regular breaths laden with warmth and sweetness. Her hair lay straggling behind her in a pigtail and when he leant close to her, it delicately tickled him. He bent over her and saw right down into her blouse where her breasts were pressed together into a cleft around which they rose in two soft mounds of abundant flesh. He sighed and laid his lips into the back of her neck. He had to shut his eyes, the sensation was so unutterably sweet to him. His hand groped down into her blouse, but suddenly she jerked away from him and muttered, 'Leave me alone.' He turned back into his own part of the bed and did not feel so good any more.

Next morning it appeared they were not on speaking terms. He had forgotten all about her quarrel with him but she, he now found out, had not. When she served his breakfast, she did so with a defiant little slam. He looked up in surprise, but saw only her retreating back with the pigtail swinging aggressively. After a while he made an excuse to talk to her. He followed her into the kitchen where she squatted stirring something in the fire. 'The puris were very good this morning,' he said sheepishly. It was the first time he had ever praised her cooking, but she gave no indication of having heard. Only her lips tightened, and she leant forward to peer into the pot in which she was stirring. Prem waited a bit longer, but finally saw nothing for it but to leave for college. He was about to go down the stairs, when a voice hissed behind him. 'Bibiji's puris are always very good.' He turned round and there was the servant-boy glaring at him with angry eyes.

So all morning he thought more about Indu than he did about the swami. He wondered what he could do to placate her. Perhaps, he thought, he should bring her some present. Only he did not know what she would like. He might have consulted Sohan Lal if, after yesterday's visit, he had not felt a little ashamed to show his concern over these trivial worldly matters. But he could not help being concerned: he wanted Indu to think kindly of him again. He had had no experience of giving presents to women, and the only thing he could think of that might please her was a sari. But that took rather more money than he at present had. He had still not decided on anything when he went home at midday. On the way, as he went through the bazaar, he passed a sweetmeat stall where people stood outside drinking frothy buttermilk out of tall, brass tumblers or eating sweetmeats, swimming in syrup, out of earthenware pots. Prem made his selection of sweetmeats and spent rather more than he could afford.

But when he got home, he did not know how to present his gift to her. His lunch was served to him with the same slam as his breakfast had been, and she walked away with the same swing of her hips and of her pigtail. Afterwards, though, he followed her into the bedroom and, holding out the earthenware pot of sweetmeats to her, he said in a shy appealing voice, 'I brought this for you.'

She gave one short look, then turned away again. She said, 'I don't want.'

'Take it,' Prem urged, going one step nearer and still holding it out to her.

After a while she said 'What is it?'

'Sweetmeats,' he replied eagerly. 'Rasgullas and gulab jamuns and jelabis . . .'

'All right. Give it.'

She sat down on the edge of the bed and at once began to eat. He watched her, first with gratification then with surprise at the amount and speed with which she was eating. She finished each sweetmeat in two neat bites, then at once fished for another one. In between she licked her lips and her finger-tips with a pink and greedy little tongue.

He said, 'You are very hungry?'

'No,' she said. 'But I long for sweetmeats. I long and long and long for them,' she said passionately, fishing out another one.

He sat down beside her on the bed. 'Why didn't you tell me before? I would have brought for you'; and when she merely shrugged in reply added, 'You must tell me everything.'

'You want?' she said and held out a piece of rasgulla, wet and wounded where she had just bitten into it. He opened his mouth and allowed her to lay it on his tongue, managing to lick her fingers before she withdrew them.

'If you don't tell me, how am I to know what you want?' he urged her. After a while a new thought struck him, 'You don't feel ill any time?' he anxiously asked; and when she shook her head, 'Or do you have a pain – here?' he whispered, shyly pointing at that part of her where she was carrying her baby.

'No no,' she laughed. 'Only I want to eat sweetmeats all the time.'

'Every day I will bring for you.' Midday heat lay hot and close in the room. Indu smelt of perspiration and a very sweet scent, rather like vanilla essence, which she used.

'Please take them away from me,' she begged, giving him the earthenware pot in which there were now only a few sweetmeats left.

'Eat eat,' he said indulgently. He took out another sweetmeat and offered it to her between finger and thumb. 'No,' she said. 'Yes,' he said, and gently forced it between her lips. She ate with relish, moaning. 'I have had too many already.' He kissed her cheek and then her neck. She did not push him away, nor did he feel at all ashamed, though it was daytime.

Then there was a loud knock on the outer door and a voice called 'Telegram!' Prem started up and took it and tore it open. He went back into the bedroom and told her: 'My mother is coming this evening on the Punjab Mail.'

'Oh,' she said. And he, too, to his surprise, found he was not as pleased as he thought he would have been.

2

'Be careful with that jar,' Prem's mother said. 'It is your favourite pickle.' Prem smiled rather sheepishly, and helped her to climb into the tonga. 'Are all my things here?' she asked. 'They won't fall out?' She had a lot of baggage: there was a steel trunk with a big padlock to it, a roll of bedding, a great number of cloth bundles tied with thick string, a basket and an earthenware water-container. Prem did his best to accommodate all these things safely in the tonga, while the tonga-driver sat perched up on his seat, with his whip in his hand, and watched him. The horse stood with its head patiently lowered and the porter stood waiting for his money.

At last they started off and Prem's mother asked, 'How much did you pay him?' When Prem told her, she said, 'That is too much. I never give more than two annas to a porter. They don't expect more.' Prem said nothing, only lowered his eyes as if he felt the justice of her rebuke. 'You must learn not to be extravagant,' she said. 'Now that you will soon have a family of your own.'

When they got home, she looked Indu up and down. 'You don't show,' she said, almost accusingly.

Indu turned away her face and drew up her sari to hide her bashful look. Prem hovered around them; he felt nervous, without quite knowing why.

Prem's mother sighed and said, 'May it be a healthy boy.'

A string-cot had been put up for her in the living-room, and she had soon accommodated herself, her steel trunk, her earthenware water-container and her basket. She sat on the bed and began to untie her many cloth bundles. There were Prem's favourite biscuits, pickles, chutneys, guava cheese, sherbet – all of which she had made at home for him before she came. As she unpacked and displayed them, she sighed, 'I know how much you like these things.' Her sigh at once made clear the infinite labour she had undergone in the preparation of them.

Indu went to bed early. Prem was tired and would have liked to follow her soon after, but his mother had a lot to tell him. She gave him all the news about his four sisters and complained about her four sons-in-law. One did not earn enough, another spent too much time at the Club, the third expected his wife to massage his legs every evening, the fourth made too many children. All of them were lacking in respect towards their mother-in-law. 'If your father had been alive,' she kept saying, 'things would have been different'; and she wiped her eyes with a corner of her sari.

Prem's sisters were all considerably older than he was, and though he was fond of them, he was not as interested in their affairs as his mother's lengthy recital assumed. On the other hand, he very much wanted to know about some other aspects of his Ankhpur life, but when he asked about these, she was not able to give him any information. 'And Rajinder – he is still in his uncle's business?' 'Have they made Ganpat's marriage yet?' 'Has the new cinema been opened?' 'Who has replaced Mr Williams as station-master?' To almost every question he asked, she pursed her mouth and said, 'What do I know of these things?'

Besides his sisters and their families, the only other topic on which she cared to dwell was that of Ankhpur College and its Principal. 'Things are becoming worse and worse,' she reported. 'He is ruining that college. All your father's lifework he is undoing.' Prem shook his head and tried to look troubled. Though really he had never had much affection for Ankhpur College. It was housed in a grim nineteenth-century Gothic building which had once been the municipal offices, and its main purpose was to turn out graduates to fill the lower-rank posts in the U.P. Civil Service. 'Just think,' his mother said, 'in this year's B.A. results there was no one in the first division and only four students in the second division!' Prem clicked his tongue, as seemed expected of him. 'What sort of man is he to replace your father?' his mother demanded. 'And his wife . . .' Here she had a lot more to say. Prem did not listen very carefully. He was wondering when she would allow him to go to bed. Indu was probably asleep by now. At last his mother said, 'Come, son, I have had a tiring journey.' Prem left her and lay down next to Indu in their bedroom. He fell asleep in a somewhat gloomy state of mind.

The following night Indu again went to bed much earlier than she usually did. As soon as she had gone, Prem's mother said in a flat and melancholy way, 'She seems a good girl.' Prem made no comment; as a matter of fact, he felt very much embarrassed and pretended that there was something wrong with the leg of the little cane table which urgently needed his attention.

'I did my best for you, son,' his mother said with a sigh. 'If your father had been alive, perhaps . . .' and she gave another deeper sigh. Prem turned the table right round and hit at its leg with the flat of his hand.

'Her family could have given you some more things,' she said. 'Look at this room – how bare it is . . .'

Prem mumbled, 'They have given us a bed.'

'*One* bed,' his mother said. She added, 'It is not as if the girl is very pretty.' Prem bent his head lower to hide his flushed face. What could he say?

'And she is not very much educated,' his mother said. She scratched under her bun of hair with her finger-nail, then looked at the finger-nail as if she expected to find something in it. 'She is not even very good at household duties.'

Prem said in a strangled voice, 'I think I will go to bed. I have to get up early in the morning.'

'My poor son. You work so hard.' She heaved another sigh. 'God's will,' she said, and laid herself sadly to sleep.

Prem very much wanted to say something to Indu. She seemed to be asleep, but he hoped that she was only pretending. 'Listen,' he urgently whispered, and when there was no response: 'Listen, it is very important.' 'What?' she whispered back, rather suspiciously. He tried to think what he could tell her that was of any importance. 'You have not forgotten Sunday the fourth,' he finally said.

'What?' she said sleepily.

'Sunday the fouth – the Principal's tea-party.'

'You have woken me up because of that?'

'You don't understand – it is very important. You see, we must make a good impression so that Mr Khanna will give us – '

'Please let me sleep.'

'Listen to me.'

'Son?' inquired Prem's mother from the living-room. Prem sank back on to the pillow. Indu flung herself to the extreme edge of the bed, where she again pretended to be asleep.

'Son? Is something wrong?' Prem shut his eyes and kept silent. 'Shall I come, son?'

'We are sleeping, Mother!'

There was a slight mutter from the living-room, then silence. Prem did not dare talk again to Indu. He could only lie there, feeling guilty towards her; he knew he should have said something to his mother to let her know that Indu was not such an inferior girl as she seemed to suppose.

With his mother staying there, the atmosphere in his small flat became rather strained. It seemed to him that both his mother and Indu were waiting for him to resolve the strain, but this he always failed to do. It was so unpleasant for him that, if he had had somewhere else to go, he would never have come home in the evenings. So that he looked forward quite eagerly to Saturday, which was the day Hans and Kitty were going to take him to a party.

But it turned out not to be a real party at all. By party Prem understood some kind of festivity – a wedding, a name-giving ceremony, a Puja celebration– with fairy lights in the trees and auspicious banana-leaves, and marigold garlands; with sweetmeats oozing syrup and ghee, and excited children, and shouting and laughing and music and spontaneous singing, and bejewelled women shimmering in satin with jasmine in their hair. But there was nothing like that at this party. It was out in the garden, but no one had bothered to put up any pretty decorations. People sat on cane-bottomed chairs with high stiff backs to them, and all anyone did was talk. There were a great many middle-aged European ladies. Some of them had Indian husbands with them, who sat staid and subdued on the chairs while their wives ran about and eagerly talked. Others had no husbands, but they had all, Prem gathered, been in India a long time. They were worn-looking ladies in floral frocks which did not fit very well and from out of which came pallid white legs with blue veins on them. When they talked, they interspersed the flow of rapid English with a number of Hindustani words, which they pronounced fluently enough but with a strange accent.

Both Hans and Kitty seemed to enjoy themselves tremendously. Both of them were too busy to take much notice of Prem, who was consequently left sitting unintroduced on a hard-backed chair by himself. From time to time Hans threw himself on to the chair next to him, which was mostly left vacant, shouting, 'I have just had the most marvellous conversation!' But he never had time to explain what it was about, for he soon caught sight of someone else he wanted to talk to and jumped up with a great bound to join them. Prem could see him talking emphatically and with many gestures, from time to time wiping the saliva from his lips which had gathered there in the excitement.

'Having a nice time, dear?' Kitty asked Prem absentmindedly, as she passed near him, deep in conversation with another lady. He stumbled hastily to his feet and said, 'Thank you, I am enjoying very much.'

'Isn't he a nice boy,' Kitty said. 'Well dear, if you like, we'll have a discussion on it next week.'

'Of course it *must* be discussed,' the lady said earnestly. She had big teeth like a horse and a long neck thrust slightly forward round which she wore a bead necklace.

'The soul must be aired, so to speak,' Kitty said. She turned to Prem: 'Don't you think so, dear?'

'Who is he?' the lady with the bead necklace inquired, looking keenly at Prem who shuffled his feet and smiled ingratiatingly.

'Ever such a nice boy,' Kitty said.

'Is he aware?' asked the lady with the necklace.

'Oh, I should think so. He's ever such a – there's a sandwich crumb on your lip, dear,' she told Prem, who hastily began to brush at his mouth.

The lady thrust her head forward at Prem and told him, almost viciously, 'You may be Indian by birth, but we are all Indian by conviction.' She pulled back her head and looked complacent.

'Marvellous!' cried Hans who now came up to join them. 'How well you spoke it: Indian by conviction.'

Prem cleared his throat and began to speak. 'All through our long struggle for Independence, our convictions – '

'Don't drag politics into it!' cried the lady. 'What does it matter, Independence or no Independence?' Prem was horrified. Was she suggesting that India should not be free? All his patriotism bristled up.

'Can anyone rule the spirit except the Self?' the lady fiercely demanded, stretching wide her blurred yellowish eyes as if to make them flash.

'Bravo!' cried Hans, clapping his hands together.

'Afghans, Moghuls, British, Hindus — what does it matter who rules the body of India? Her soul is always free and calm and lost in contemplation of the Self.'

Hans was radiant with delight. He looked with eager eyes from the lady's face into Prem's, as if he were now expecting the latter to retort with something equally forceful. But Prem did not know what to say. Nevertheless Hans exclaimed: 'What marvellous discussion we are having!'

'How sick I am of petty politicians!' the lady cried, glaring at Prem.

Kitty said, 'It does seem awfully like putting the cart before the horse, doesn't it?'

'Horse?' said Hans.

The lady gave an indignant tug at her necklace: 'Politics are all very well for other, materialistic countries, but here first things come first.'

Prem cleared his throat. 'A nation must be free,' he said and thought he tried to speak up bravely, his voice came out timid and rather squeaky.

'No dear,' Kitty said, laying a kind hand on his arm. 'That's not quite what we're talking about.'

The lady shut her eyes and said, 'What's the use of talking to people like that.' Prem realized that he was creating a poor impression and that made him feel very bad.

'I will explain,' Hans said. 'Prem, you see that none of us are Indian by birth but we are all here. Why?'

'You had a dream,' Prem murmured.

'Quite right!' Hans cried. He held up a forefinger in the air and seemed pleased. 'I had a dream — "Come, Hans," the swami said. But there are others who had no dream. They came to this India, perhaps for business, perhaps for studies. They thought it was only for a short time, but they also had to stay. They know only in India they who find themselves.'

'The thing is to become com*plete*,' the lady with the necklace said. To give the last word special emphasis she drew back her lips and bared her long yellow teeth. And then, to Prem's surprise, she stretched her mouth wider, revealing more teeth; she was smiling, and not only smiling, but smiling at Prem. She said archly, 'Perhaps you are complete already.'

'He does look a nice boy,' Kitty said.

Hans threw his arm round Prem's shoulder: 'The first time I met him he was in contemplation. Yes, yes,' he cried at Prem, 'don't try to deny, you were sitting there on the park-bench lost in contemplation – I could see from your eyes.' He squeezed Prem's shoulder affectionately: 'I am proud you are my friend.' Prem did not feel as stirred by these last words as he should have done. When Hans said 'friend', Prem thought of Raj, and he wished he were with Raj.

'I must go home now, please,' he murmured. Nobody heard him, for they had all turned away to listen to a wizened white lady in a cotton sari, who was recounting her experiences with a very advanced yogi in Lucknow.

When it was their day for meeting, Raj again failed to turn up. After waiting for a considerable time in the vestibule of the cinema, Prem began to think that perhaps something was wrong with Raj or his family – why else should Raj neglect to meet his only Ankhpur friend? The more he thought about it, the more he became convinced that something untoward was preventing Raj from keeping his appointment. He resolved instantly to go and see him.

It took him a long time on the bus to get there, and when he did arrive, it was difficult for him to find the house, for he had never been there before. It was in a large colony of houses for Grade Three Civil Servants. There were rows and rows of hutments, each one with an oval door, a little veranda and a tiny rectangle of grass in front. It was evening, so all the doors were open and the men sat outside, relaxing after their day in the office, neat, thin, earnest clerks off-duty in vests and dhotis. There were many children running around, playing and shouting and throwing balls; a triangle of grass had been converted into a playground for them, and here they swung on shabby swings or turned slowly and with an air of boredom on a creaking roundabout. There was also a row of shops, a chemist, a dry-cleaner lit up by neon-lighting, a grocer with rice and lentils and red chillies kept in tall tins, a barber and a dried-fruits store. A radio played loud wailing music from out of the barber's shop.

Raj sat outside his hutment, looking very much like all the other clerks sitting outside their hutments. He too was wearing a vest and a dhoti. He was trying to read the morning's paper but was distracted from this by a little girl who kept plucking at the grass and falling over. 'Come here, Babli!' Raj called in an anxious voice. He ran after the little girl and picked her up and then carefully dusted the earth from her knickers. He was engaged in this when he looked up and saw Prem. He became frozen for a moment, then hastily put his child down. He did not seem at all pleased to see Prem; on the contrary, he even looked rather sulky. Prem felt as if he had gone to see a stranger, and not his friend Raj at all.

'I was waiting for you in the cinema,' Prem said. But seeing Raj's frown deepen, he was afraid that this might sound like a reproach, so he added hastily: 'I thought perhaps you were ill, that is why I –'

'There has been great pressure of work in my office,' Raj said. 'You can have no idea how work piles up in a Government office.' He put his hand to his forehead to indicate the load of work he was made to sustain.

Prem smiled at the little girl and beckoned to her with his hand. But she hid behind her father's dhoti and hung on to his leg. 'She is shy with strangers,' Raj said. 'One day your boss in the office will decide that certain inventories in File G must now be classified with other inventories in File M. Then there is one mad rush all day to get together all the inventories from File G – you can sit down if you like,' he said, pointing to the basket-chair in which his opened newspaper still lay crumbled; 'rest for a moment.' He turned his head and called into the house: 'Bring the other chair!'

Prem removed and carefully folded Raj's paper and sat down. A moment later a stout square woman, in a blue cotton sari with a red border to it tucked round her waist, carried out another basket-chair. Prem assumed that she was Raj's wife, but as no attempt at introduction was made, he pretended not to see her. She stood for a moment in the oval of the door, scratching her elbow and staring at Prem, before disappearing again inside.

'Come, I will show you someting nice,' Prem said to the little girl. He took his handkerchief and wound it round his finger, making it look like a Sikh wearing a turban.

'My brother-in-law has already shown her that trick,' Raj said. 'In our office a departmental note may come at three o'clock in the afternoon to say that seventeen copies of a notice must be instantly typed and dispatched.' He laughed dryly: 'That is how it is in Government service.'

'What do you call her?'

'Her pet name is Babli. People like you who have never held a Government post can have no idea what it is like.'

'You won't come to me, Babli?' Prem smiled and patted his lap.

'It is hell,' Raj said with satisfaction. 'But what to do? If one has a family to support, one cannot pick and choose, one must work, work, work at one's job.'

'Do you go to school, Babli?'

'She is only two. This is another worry we shall have to face next year – the school fees that have to be paid every month. It is a great burden.' The little girl rubbed herself against his legs and he absent-mindedly stroked her head. Prem suddenly realized that it would not be long before he too had a child, and this thought made him so unexpectedly happy that he was quite embarrassed. To hide this, he bent down from his chair and plucked at some blades of grass.

Raj's wife came out with a tea-tray, which she placed with a lot of clatter on to a footstool. She did not go away but stood watching them, with one arm akimbo. She was a rather plain woman and, though still young, already much too fat.

'Are you comfortable in this place?' Prem asked. Since Raj was ignoring his wife, Prem could only follow suit.

'What to do?' said Raj. 'Beggars can't be choosers.'

'What – comfortable!' Raj's wife surprisingly interposed. She spoke with heat and in a somewhat raucous voice. 'Have you seen the state of this place? It is falling in ruins about our heads!'

'Yes, yes,' Raj said irritably, 'now don't talk so loud.'

'All the ceilings are cracked, and when it rains, the water comes into the house like a flood.'

'It is allotted to us by Government,' Raj said. 'Naturally we have to take what we are given. And the rent is not so bad.' He fed sugar to his child from a spoon, which she licked with relish.

'The W.C. was broken a long time ago, so that we have to use a commode,' Raj's wife said.

'All right, all right,' Raj said to her over his shoulder.

'And the sweeper comes only twice a day to clean it out. It is very inconvenient for us. When you have finished with the tea, I will take away the tray.' She bent down to pick it up. Though he tried modestly not to look at her, Prem could not help noticing that she was clumsy in her movements. She dropped things and bumped her elbow and when she walked, she placed her feet in square heavy thuds. Prem thought of Indu, of her light swift ways, and felt rather pleased.

Prem said, 'My mother has come from Ankhpur, and is staying with us.'

Raj gave him a swift look. 'Everything is all right?'

'How do you mean?' Prem said with an uneasy laugh.

Raj shook his head. 'I know it is often difficult when a wife and a mother meet.' He gave a sigh, which seemed to come from out of the memory of a deep experience. Prem looked at him with respect. He felt there was much he could learn from Raj.

'One day you must come to my house also,' he said. 'You and your wife. And of course Babli must not be left at home.' He tried to chuck the child under the chin but she quickly hid her head behind her arms. 'We can all meet together for a meal at my house.' He rather like the prospect of entertaining Raj and his family. There was something solid and respectable about a family party, which appealed to him more now than meeting only Raj in the vestibule of the cinema.

When he got home, he found his mother alone. She was sitting on her bed; she had not turned the light on. 'Your wife is downstairs,' she said bitterly.

'With the Seigals?'

'How do I know what their name is?'

'I will go and fetch her.' He walked away rather hastily.

'The servant also is not here!' She called after him. 'There is no one to make even a cup of tea for me!'

He clicked his tongue. 'At once I will fetch her.' He ran quickly down the stairs. There were several visitors in the Seigals' house. Mr Seigal sat with three other men at a little card-table which had been placed right under the ceiling fan. They were arguing loudly about something and seemed to be quite angry. Romesh lay on the sofa, as indolently as if he were floating in a boat, his hand trailing on the carpet and his eyes fixed dreamily into the distance. Indu was out on the veranda with some other ladies. She was helping Mrs Seigal to wind wool and looked quite happy and smiling. When she saw Prem, though, her face changed and she became passive and expressionless. He noticed this, and was hurt.

He declined to sit down. 'My mother is waiting for us,' he told Mr Seigal. Indu followed him with obvious reluctance. At the bottom of the stairs, he asked her in a hurried low voice, 'What happened?'

'Nothing happened.'

'Why did you leave my mother all alone?'

She shrugged and walked up the stairs. He came behind her, feeling uneasy and unhappy. They had hardly entered when Prem's mother began to complain: 'What sort of a household is it, where the servant is out, the wife is out, the mother who has come to visit is left alone without tea and sitting in darkness?' Prem switched the light on with a sharp click. 'It is hurting my eyes!' his mother cried. Indu had quietly slipped into the kitchen and was lighting the fire.

'I am sorry for you, son,' Prem's mother said. 'When I am not here, there is no one to look after your comforts. My poor boy, to have to work so hard and then to come home to an empty house with the fire unlit, no tea, no light, nothing. Thank God I always knew what my duty was towards your father. *He* never had to come home to such a house.' The servant-boy could be heard singing as he came up the stairs. Prem ran out and seized him by the shoulder. 'Where have you been?' Prem shouted.

The boy looked at him in astonishment. His mouth was open, interrupted in mid-song. 'Where have you been?' Prem shouted and he gave the boy's shoulder a shake which, however, in contrast to his fierce voice, was rather feeble.

'Son!' Prem's mother called from the sitting-room. 'Don't upset yourself, son!'

Indu came out of the kitchen. The boy looked at her and asked: 'What is the matter with him?'

Prem let go of his shoulder and turned indignantly to Indu. 'What a rude undisciplined boy he is.'

'Don't upset yourself, son! You will make yourself ill!'

Suddenly Indu was shouting at the servant-boy: 'You son of the devil, you little pig, where have you been?' She advanced in a threatening attitude, swaggering slightly, with arms akimbo and her fists pushed against her hips. 'Just wait till I – ' The boy ducked and fled into the kitchen. She followed him: 'I will tear out your eyes and stamp on them . . .' Prem went back into the sitting-room. His mother was still sitting on her bed; she was combing her hair and had hairpins in her mouth. They could hear Indu shouting in the kitchen: 'I will batter in your teeth and twist off your ears!' Prem's mother took the hairpins out of her mouth and said, 'She has bad temper also. My poor son.'

*

Indu did not again object to accompanying Prem to Mr Khanna's tea-party. On the contrary, she seemed quite glad to go, as if she were glad to escape from the house for an afternoon. She spent a long time dressing herself. Prem watched her and was fascinated. She wore one of her best saris, one that had been given her on her marriage – a lilac-coloured georgette with big flowers and leaves stitched on it in imitation pearls. With that she wore red shoes which had high platform soles and cut-out toes. She also put on her jewellery – a heavy gold necklace and long ear-rings and twelve gold bangles – smoothed and liberally oiled her hair and wound it round with a fresh chain of jasmine, applied the red mark on her forehead and finally even a little lipstick on her lips. How different she looked from the everyday Indu, who wore cotton saris tucked round her waist, glass bangles and usually no shoes at all. Prem gazed at her in admiration. Her eyes were shining, and her lipstick, her gold, her jasmine, her hair-oil all gave her an almost opulent effect. Prem's mother said, 'You children can go and enjoy yourselves. I will be here to guard everything.'

Prem was wearing his best shirt and trousers, and he felt proud as they walked together to the college. For a time they did not speak. Indu was concentrating on her walking, which was a little difficult for her owing to her unaccustomed high platform soles. Prem too was rather self-conscious and walked in a slow and stately way. They were very obviously two people dressed up in their best clothes and going somewhere special.

After a while Indu said, 'What shall I do if someone speaks to me there?'

'Of course you must answer very politely and also in such a way that people can see that you are educated.'

Indu kept silent. Prem glanced at her out of the corner of his eyes and saw that she was looking worried: she was biting her lip and frowning. He realized she was thinking how difficult it would be to answer in such a way. He also began to worry and hoped that she would show herself to her best advantage.

It was strange to see the college downstairs so empty. 'This is my classroom,' he whispered to her as they passed, but she hardly turned her head. She was biting her lip quite hard. Upstairs in Mr Khanna's living-room members of the staff and their wives, all dressed up in their best, were already seated in a pre-arranged circle of chairs. Mr Khanna was standing in the centre; he was talking, and there was a polite titter of laughter in response. When he saw Prem and Indu, he called in a hearty cheery voice: 'Yes, come in, come in!' Even Mrs Khanna smiled a welcome at them. Everyone's attention was drawn to the new arrivals, chairs were shifted to accommodate them and Mr Khanna said in a loud hospitable tone, 'Please be quite comfortable!' Indu kept her eyes lowered and her face looked quite swollen with embarrassment. Prem kept saying 'Thank you'.

'As I was saying,' said Mr Khanna; he took up his position in the centre again and replaced his thumb in his armpit. 'It is very pleasant to have the ladies with us. Very agreeable.' The ladies all stared straight in front of them, without any change of expression. Only Mrs Khanna said, 'I think the tea-water is nearly boiling.'

Mr Chaddha said, 'The society of ladies is said to have a very softening effect.' He was wearing a cream-coloured silk suit which seemed to have been washed quite a number of times, and he sat with his arms and his little bird legs crossed in an attitude of ease suitable to a tea-party.

'It is not for nothing,' suggested Mr Khanna, 'that they are known as the gentle sex.' Led by Mr Chaddha, the gentlemen politely laughed. 'It is good sometimes to break off in the midst of toil,' Mr Khanna continued, 'and enjoy an hour's leisure and ease in their charming company.'

'As our heroes of old,' said Mr Chaddha, 'withdrew for respite from their battles to have their wounds dressed and their brows soothed by the hands of their consorts.' He seemed pleased by this remark; he cleared his throat and crossed his legs the other way. The other teachers looked at the Principal, and when they saw him smile in appreciation, they too smiled in appreciation.

The ladies remained unmoved. They were all seated together in one half of the circle of chairs, while their husbands were segregated in the other half. They held themselves stiff and looked very much aware both of the clothes they were wearing, which were all shining and new, and of the opulent surroundings in which they found themselves – the armchairs, the flowered cushions and curtains, the bright paper flowers in silver vases, the coloured parchment lampshades with long tassels. Only Mrs Khanna was at ease, in clothes more gorgeous than anyone else's – wide silk pyjama trousers with a sky-blue shimmering shirt over them patterned all over with vast sprays of lilac on red stems; from time to time she gave a proprietory pat to a cushion or straightened a silver-framed photograph of Mr Khanna at an academic function.

'Relaxation is necessary to the human mind as well as to the human body,' said Mr Khanna. 'It is like a cool shower-bath we take on a hot day.' Prem gave a polite laugh, but as no one else laughed, he realized that the remark had not been humorous. He brushed imaginary specks of dust from his knee. 'Refreshed and revived,' said the Principal, 'we then resume our everyday duties with new vigour. I think we are all ready now for the tasty dishes which Mrs Khanna has prepared.'

Mrs Khanna ceremoniously handed to each guest a quarter-plate of flowered English crockery. Everyone sat and held it and patiently waited. In due course dishes of fritters, samusas and sweetmeats were circulated. The ladies were at first so shy that they simply passed them on, without taking anything, so that even when the dishes had gone full circle, the ladies still sat there holding their empty crockery plates. 'Come come,' Mr Khanna humourously rallied them, 'our ladies must show a better appetite.' So then they slipped something on to their plates as the dishes passed them, but hastily and furtively as if they wished neither to see nor to be seen. There was silence while all the guests stared into space and chewed as delicately as they could. Only Mr and Mrs Khanna ate with a really hearty appetite.

When everyone had eaten the correct amount sanctioned by good breeding, the servant went round and collected the empty plates. Soon only Mr and Mrs Khanna were left with plates. Prem wiped crumbs from his lips with his handkerchief and glanced vaguely round the circle of chairs. He did not want to look at Indu too directly, not so that anyone would notice, but he did just want to see whether everything was all right and she was behaving with the requisite decorum. When, however, his eyes finally reached her, he saw that she still had her plate; and not only did she still have her plate, but she also had rather more sweetmeats on it that was quite correct; and these sweetmeats she was eating with the same concentration and relish she had shown that day sitting on her bed when he had brought some for her in an earthenware pot. He looked away again hastily. He felt very uneasy.

'Well,' said Mr Chaddha, planting his hands on his knees and shifting forward on his chair. Everyone looked at him. 'Well,' said Mr Chaddha, 'I think we all enjoyed that very much.'

There was a murmur of assent. 'Excellent,' said one; 'a very good tea,' said another.

'We owe a profound debt of gratitude to our host and hostess,' Mr Chaddha said.

Prem's eyes stole round to Indu again. She had thrust her head forward to take bites out of a sweetmeat which she held between forefinger and thumb in a rather predatory manner.

'Not only for the sumptuous fare they so generously provided,' Mr Chaddha said, 'But also for giving us the opportunity to have this pleasant social gathering.' Again there was polite assent. Mr and Mrs Khanna put aside their plates and arranged themselves in attentively listening attitudes.

'Such gatherings,' said Mr Chaddha, 'are conducive to goodwill and good fellowship among the members of staff of Khanna Private College.'

Indu was busily licking her fingers. Only one sweetmeat was left on her plate. The servant came to collect the dishes, but before he could remove them, Indu had quickly taken two more large sweetmeats. Prem's gaze roved frantically round the circle. Everyone seemed to be looking at Mr Chaddha.

'Though daily we toil side by side,' said Mr Chaddha, 'yet to develop a proper sense of comradeship we need sometimes to share our moments of ease and leisure too.'

It was evident to Prem that Indu was by this time quite lost to her surroundings. She was continually biting, chewing, licking her fingers or flicking crumbs from her lips with her tongue. She seemed in a trance of enjoyment. He did not blame her, for he had heard that pregnant women had strange and uncontrollable desires. But he was terrified that others, who did not know of this extenuating circumstance, would notice.

For it is indeed imperative,' said Mr Chaddha, now leaning back, folding his hands over his stomach and looking up at the ceiling, 'that a sense of comradeship should be fostered among us.'

If only he could give her some sign. But she was sitting too far away and was too engrossed to look up and meet his eye. Nor could he transmit a message through anyone else. His only possible ally there was Sohan Lal, and Sohan Lal, he saw, was following Mr Chaddha's words with close attention; he had his hands clasped on his knee, his head to one side and a somewhat strained look on his face. He looked very different from the way he had done when they had gone to see the swami.

'A sense of comradeship, moreover,' said Mr Chaddha, 'that will survive and triumph over any buffets of fortune that it might be our fate to encounter.'

'Very well said!' Mr Khanna interposed. Others murmured in echo. Prem was afraid it might be noticed he was not paying close attention, so he called rather more loudly than anyone else, 'Bravo!' and even clapped his hands. But when people looked at him, he stopped clapping.

'The true value of human intercourse,' said Mr Chaddha, 'lies in the sense of loyalty that is fostered.'

'True,' said Mr Khanna, sagely nodding his head.

The servant came back to clear the remainder of the tea-things away. Mrs Khanna beckoned to him and pointed out some crumbs that had fallen on to the carpet. Prem sat forward in his seat and twisted his hands in anxiety. The servant bent down to pick the crumbs, one by one, from the carpet, while Mrs Khanna watched him sternly. Indu ate and ate. 'And not only loyalty,' Mr Chaddha said, beating both fists in the air for emphasis, 'but also reverence, courage and conviction!'

Prem glanced again around the circle. The ladies all sat with their hands in their laps, staring in front of them with solemn faces. Their husbands were eagerly craning forward to listen to Mr Chaddha. The servant had not reached the place where Indu was sitting. Here there were many more crumbs than anywhere else. Mrs Khanna frowned and her eyes travelled upward to Indu, who was just pushing the remnant of a crumbly ladoo into her mouth. Prem watched and could do nothing. Indu looked up, straight into Mrs Khanna's disapproving face. The two fingers with which she was pushing in the ladoo remained poised against her lips. Mrs Khanna pointed at Indu and said to the servant in a whisper which everyone could hear. 'There is one plate left over there.'

Mr Chaddha modulated his voice to one of softness and affection. 'What more beautiful feeling can there be than that of friendship?' he asked and held out a rhetorically appealing hand. The other lecturers breathed a long-drawn 'Ah' in appreciation. Prem's 'Ah' came a little later; all his feelings were with Indu, but he did not want to be left out of anything. He leant forward in his chair and pretended to be intent on Mr Chaddha. Yet he thought more about how he would like to explain the situation to Mrs Khanna, so that she would not think Indu had never been to a tea-party before and did not know how to behave in society. He wanted to make her understand that Indu's odd behaviour was due not to lack of breeding but to natural causes.

Mrs Khanna said, 'It is seven o'clock already.' Everybody stood up.

The tea-party was over, but Prem did not want it to be over. There still remained so much to do. He wished desperately to make some contribution to the conversation, to distinguish himself and show everyone that he was an intelligent and deep-thinking young man. But the guests were already leaving, filing past Mr Khanna who stood at the door with his hands folded in an attitude of gracious hospitality. Prem wanted to call out 'Stop!' and then as everybody turned round to look at him, begin to address them with something so poignant and striking that even those who had already gone down the stairs would be called back again. But he did not have the courage to call out, and besides, he could not really think of anything poignant and striking to say.

Though next morning he could think of plenty. How he wished then that he had had the courage to get up and make a speech, like Mr Chaddha! While he was shaving he outlined this speech which he should have made and even watched himself in the mirror making it. He spoke with a mixture of courteous flattery and touching sentiment. But it was too late. This sense of having missed an opportunity not likely to occur again greatly depressed him. Life, he thought, offers us so few chances to prove our worth. It was bitter to reflect that he had passed one by.

He spoke to Sohan Lal about his sense of failure. He said, 'It is difficult for a young man to show off his best qualities before his superiors.'

Sohan Lal did not enter on the subject with enthusiasm. It was evident that he had himself given up any ambition he may ever have had to shine, and consequently did not share Prem's sense of dissatisfaction at the silent and undistinguished role they had both played at the tea-party. Prem did not know whether to blame or admire him for his lack of ambition. On the one hand, of course, lack of ambition was a very good thing, meaning renunciation of the things of this world and the concentration of the spirit on exalted matters; but on the other hand, a man must – as Prem's father had taught him – strive and strive and strive again to reach a high and worthy position in life. Sohan Lal, it was evident, had given up hope and perhaps even desire for such position; yet his was not a true renunciation. Prem remembered the expression of anxious deference his face had worn at the tea-party and, in contrast, his gaiety and carefree abandon when they had gone to see the swami. Why, if he had truly renounced, should he be anxious to please Mr Khanna?

And here Prem came up against an inconsistency in his own attitude as well. When he remembered the swami – the happy young men, the flower garlands, the songs of praise – and the sense of exhilaration and even of release which he himself had experienced there, then his eagerness to show himself in a good light before Mr and Mrs Khanna in order to get an increase in salary, or to secure and improve his position in the college, or whatever it was he wanted from them – all that seemed futile and meaningless. But, though he realized it to be so, nevertheless his mind always tilted back again to these things. It was as if he had been turned into the light only of his own free will to swivel back to darkness.

Why had he not gone back to the swami? He had been so happy there and had promised, and really wanted, to go every day. It would cost him nothing to go, nobody asked him not to go, he would be gay and joyful there, he knew – and yet, he did not go. He wondered whether Sohan Lal had been back since that time they had gone together. But when he asked him, Sohan Lal shook his head and looked sad. 'It is difficult for me to go,' Sohan Lal said. He said nothing more, but Prem felt that this explanation was sufficient, and indeed fitted his own case too. It was difficult, not because of lack of time or distance or of any outward circumstance; but because it was so different from what one was accustomed to. The swami seemed to ask for nothing, yet afterwards one realized that he asked for almost everything and expected one to forget, for his sake, all the things one was used to and thought important.

Prem told himself that he was not ready for that yet. Perhaps if he had been unmarried; or if his wife had not been pregnant; or if it had not been expected of him to earn a living; then perhaps it would have been easy to go to the swami and sing hymns of praise. But now he was caught up in the world. He knew it was very important for him to improve his position, and by this he meant mainly, at present, his financial position.

His thoughts turned back to the rent and the Seigals, and he knew that – if only to satisfy his own conscience – he would have to make another attack on that front. Only he felt it might be more effective if Indu were to make the attack, and he told her so. 'It will be so easy for you,' he persuaded her. 'Only while you are talking with Mrs Seigal you can tell her – ' Indu shrugged one shoulder and turned away from him. 'Why not?' he said. 'What harm will it do you?'

He spoke – as usual nowadays when he wanted to speak to her

alone – in whispers, even though he had first taken the precaution of drawing her into the bedroom and shutting the door. 'While you are having conversation together you can tell her it is difficult for my husband to pay so much rent.' Indu shook her head. 'But why not?' he urged again.

'Son!' his mother called from the next room. Prem could not help emitting a small sound of impatience, and that made Indu laugh. 'Son?'

'Yes, please!' Prem called back, rather too loudly. Indu threw the end of her sari over her face and laughed from behind it.

'What are you doing, son?' his mother asked rather plaintively.

'Nothing, Mother!' Indu rocked herself to and fro on the bed.

'Why do you leave me to sit here alone?'

'Keep quiet,' Prem urgently whispered to Indu who was making choking sounds. 'I am just coming!' he called to his mother. 'I am only changing my shirt!' Quickly he put his hand over Indu's mouth; she was squirming and puffing with laughter. 'She will hear you,' he whispered.

It was not till late in the night, till his mother was asleep, that he dared talk to Indu again about the Seigals. But the most he could persuade her to was that she would accompany him on a visit to the Seigals; she would not even promise to say anything. So he could only hope that she would be manoeuvred into a position where she would have to join him in talking.

Next evening, consequently, they both washed their faces and combed their hair very carefully and went down the stairs. Prem's mother said, 'Go, children, I am here to see to everything.' On the stairs, Prem said, 'Now please remember, you promised me.'

'What did I promise?' Indu asked indignantly.

'That you would – '

'No!'

'Sh,' Prem said, for they were quite near the Seigals' door now.

Mrs Seigal was sitting on the veranda; she was crocheting. There were neither visitors nor Mr Seigal; 'He has gone out to play cards,' she said. Romesh was in the sitting-room, ostensibly studying for his examinations, but as soon as he saw there were visitors, he came out to take part in the conversation. He stood jingling coins in his pocket and said, 'Yesterday I saw the new film at the Regal.'

'Please be quite comfortable,' Mrs Seigal said. Prem thought that maybe it was a good thing that they had found her alone; it would be easier to impress their need on her and then leave her to impress it on her husband. He only hoped that Indu would co-operate.

'It was an historical film,' Romesh said. 'The love story of Shah Jehan and Mumtaz Mahal.'

'It was good?' Indu asked.

'There was plenty of singing and dancing,' Romesh said. 'But I don't care much for historical films. I like modern films best.'

'One can learn a lot from historical films,' Indu said. Prem wished she would not encourage Romesh. He did not want to spend the evening discussing films. Mrs Seigal was not paying any attention to the conversation, but sat with her head bent over her crocheting.

'I like the smart clothes that the actors wear in modern films,' Romesh said. 'And then also the nice way their houses are furnished, and the night clubs and restaurants they go to. I don't get much chance to see what elegant life is like, that is why I am glad I can learn from films.'

Prem thought about how he could come to discuss young married life and its difficulties with Mrs Seigal. It seemed to him that the subject would be interesting to her and that she would listen with sympathy; so that he could, from there on, lead to the necessity of having a lower rent. He glanced at her out of the corner of his eye, wondering how to start off, and saw that she was crying.

'And singing and dancing I am very fond of,' Romesh said.

Prem did not know whether he should pretend he had not noticed Mrs Seigal's tears, or whether he should offer comfort to her. It was becoming difficult to ignore her. She was sniffing and dabbing at her eyes, which were red-rimmed.

'I am very fond of all comic actors,' Romesh said. 'They make me laugh a lot.'

Indu said, 'I don't like to laugh in the cinema.'

Mrs Seigal drew a closely folded letter out of the petticoat string at her waist. 'Today I had a letter from my daughter,' she said and dabbed at her eyes.

'She is well, I hope?' Indu said.

'My poor child,' Mrs Seigal said, dabbing. Prem cleared his throat whereat Indu, for some unknown reason, frowned at him, so that he dared not do it again though he felt he wanted to.

'I am also fond of very sad films which make one cry,' Romesh said.

'What can a mother do,' Mrs Seigal said. She unfolded her letter and nodded over it gloomily. 'We were so careful when we made the match.'

Indu said in a grown-up sensible voice, 'Often it is difficult to tell.'

'Did you see that film,' Romesh said, 'in which the heroine was married to a man who turned out to be the chief of a gang of gangsters? He was a proper rogue.'

'My poor daughter,' Mrs Seigal said and covered her eyes with her handkerchief. 'What can we do for her, with such a husband?' She added in a shocked whisper: 'He is a big drinker.'

Prem instantly looked serious and troubled. 'It is a very bad vice,' he said.

'Oh, my poor daughter.'

'If it is not checked in time,' Prem said gravely, 'it can lead to very serious consequences.'

'How many times have I told Mr Seigal,' Mrs Seigal said, 'go and see our daughter, see what can be done, but what is his answer to me?'

'In such cases it is the duty of the relatives to intervene,' Prem said. Indu directed a terrible frown at him. He looked down and twisted his hands and kept quiet.

'He says to me what is the use of going there? He will not even listen to me, but sits down to play cards. How selfish men are.' Indu sighed in sympathy, which made Prem give her a hurt look.

'Who else is there I can turn to? My Romesh is a good boy, but he is a child only.' Romesh looked down at his own feet and scuffed them. Then he murmured in a thick voice, 'I am eighteen.'

Indu said, 'Yes, it is often difficult for a woman to know where to turn for help and protection.' She spoke with an authority that surprised Prem and also made him feel guilty.

'We gave her such a beautiful wedding,' Mrs Seigal moaned. 'More than three hundred came.'

'There were two bands,' Romesh said. 'They played very good tunes.'

'My poor daughter, my child,' Mrs Seigal said and wept into her handkerchief.

Later that night, when they were in bed together, Indu whispered, 'Why did you not ask her about reduction in rent?'

'How could I do so,' he whispered back, 'when she was so sad?'

Indu made no reply.

'How could any person with feelings ask her at such a moment?'

'I told you not to ask.'

'But we shall have to ask! When she is feeling better, that is ... Do you realize that 45 rupees is more than one-quarter of our whole monthly salary? How can we give more than one-quarter for rent only? We will starve. Are you listening to me?'

'No, I am sleeping.'

Prem lay awake for quite a long time. He was thinking, but not of the reduction in rent he had to ask for. Instead he was thinking of Mrs Seigal and how she had dabbed at her eyes and said, 'My poor daughter.' He felt very sorry for her. How little one knows of other's sorrows, he thought. He had always regarded her as a placid, happy woman who sat crocheting on her veranda and chatted with guests amid a round of tea and sweetmeats. Now he realized that this ideal picture was not true. And he thought of how everywhere in the world it was like that, how people one thought happy all had some hidden sorrow, so that there was no happiness anywhere but only people crying alone and in secret. It is true, he thought, everything is Illusion, and this thought saddened him: yet at the same time he felt a kind of relief, for he realized that if everything was Illusion, then his own worries too were Illusion and there was no need for him to be oppressed by them.

However, his new-found sense of freedom did not last till morning, and even if he still had some slight remembrance of it when he woke up, this was quickly dispelled by the sound of his mother quarrelling. She was shouting in a shrill voice. 'Is this the respect I get in my son's house?' He got up hurriedly. Indu came running in and he asked her in a whisper, 'What has happened?' Indu shrugged and lay face-downwards on the bed. 'I have come from so far away to be with my son, and this is how I am treated!'

Prem lingered for a while. He combed his hair and stared with unhappy eyes into the mirror. Indu lay without moving on the bed; he knew from her attitude that she would not speak to him, so he asked her nothing further. He gave a last sad look into the mirror and went into the sitting-room. As soon as she saw him, his mother began to cry. He gave an inaudible sigh and then asked, 'What has happened?'

'No, son,' she sobbed. 'Why should I burden you with my troubles?'

He sat down and quietly sighed to himself again.

'It is enough that I should suffer ...'

The servant-boy came with her tea on a tray. 'I don't want it,' she said. 'I am not eating or drinking anything in this house again.'

'Put it down,' Prem told the boy.

'No, son, I will have nothing. I have been insulted in your house.'

Prem wrung his hands. 'How insulted? Who insulted you?'

'I would go out in the fields so as not to trouble anyone, but there are no fields and I must use the bathroom.'

Prem stirred her tea and said, 'Drink, you will feel better.'

'Why should she grudge me the use of the bathroom?'

'But I did not know she was in there!' Indu cried in an anguished voice from the bedroom.

'You see!' his mother said. 'You see how she shouts at me!'

Prem said, 'It was a mistake. She did not know you were in there.'

'What mistake! She grudges me the use of the bathroom, even though I have come all this way to be with my son.' She wiped her eyes with the corner of her sari. 'Get me my ticket for tomorrow night, son. I will go home. I am not welcome here.'

He handed her the tea and she drank it. When she had finished, she said, 'There is no need to take me to the station. I will find by myself. I don't wish to be a trouble to anyone'; she began to cry again.

When Prem came home at lunchtime, the atmosphere was still very strained. His mother was walking round the sitting-room, silently and with a tight-lipped look of martyrdom, ineffectively piling up a few clothes in a pretence of packing. Indu was equally silent and tight-lipped. Prem was glad to get back to the college again.

But in the evening everything was different. His mother was in the kitchen. She was cooking. 'What are you doing?' he exclaimed, quite shocked. She tilted the frying-pan in which onions were floating in clarified butter. 'Just wait, son, and see what I am cooking for you today.' She looked and sounded remarkably cheerful.

'Why are you cooking? Where is – ?'

'Bibiji has gone,' the servant-boy said. He was sitting despondently in a corner with his knees dawn up and his hair hanging over his face.

'Her uncle came for her,' Prem's mother said in the same cheerful voice as before. 'Your favourite dish I have cooked – just wait till you taste it.'

'She went away with her uncle?'

'She took a big suitcase,' the servant-boy moaned.

Prem went into the bedroom. Indu was always neat, so it did not look very different. But he noticed at once that her little wooden table on gilded lion-feet was empty of the bottle of hair-oil, the comb and the glass phial of scent she usually kept on it. The picture of Mother and Baby, which she had bought since her pregnancy, had also gone from the wall. Timidly he opened her wardrobe, but shut it again immediately for it was quite empty. He lay down on the bed and closed his eyes and stayed like that for a long time. And he would have liked to stay even longer if his mother had not called him.

She was bustling and almost cheerful, the way he remembered her as being in her own home. And she talked a lot – about his sister in Bangalore and Ankhpur College and the new Principal there. He listened quite carefully, hoping she would say something about Indu's departure, but she never did. At last he asked, 'She left no message for me?'

'What?' said his mother, her mind still back in Ankhpur.

The servant-boy, hovering in the doorway, said, 'She left just like that; without one word.'

Prem, who was sitting crosslegged on the floor, drew invisible patterns with his finger-nail on the ground before him. His mother went on talking: 'And on the Annual Day he did not hire enough chairs, so that many of the visitors had to stand.' The servant-boy said, 'I begged her to take me with her, but she would not even answer me.' 'You are sure she left no message for me? Nothing at all?' 'I told you – she left without one word.'

'Why are you talking so much?' Prem's mother scolded the servant-boy. 'Have you no work in the kitchen that you must stand here like an uncle?'

The boy went out muttering to himself. 'He is a very bad servant,' Prem's mother said severely. 'He should be told to go and a better one taken in his place.'

In the night Prem felt very much alone, even though his mother was sleeping in the next room. He wondered for how long Indu had gone away. She had taken all her things, so it looked as if she intended to stay a long time. That was another three months – and she had not even said good-bye to him, not even left a message. Suddenly he was angry. Why did she go? Who told her to go? She knew very well that he had forbidden it. Yet she had completely ignored his wishes – and not only his wishes, but even his existence; had just packed and gone off with her uncle, without leaving a message. He felt in a mood to go after her and show her how angry he was at her. He could take leave from Mr Khanna on some pretext and go off on the evening train. But when he thought of arriving at her house, and how her sisters would gape and giggle at him, and her fat merry uncles make jokes at him, and Indu herself perhaps be angry with him, he abandoned the idea. Instead he would write her a letter. A long and very angry letter.

But next day he was no longer angry. Now he was too despondent to want to write a letter. He went to the college and found everything there very depressing. Mr Chaddha was lecturing on the Portuguese and French settlements in India and his class was fervently taking notes. Prem's class sat around in easy attitudes, played the Dot-game and passed notes to one another. Everything was so very much as usual. At the morning break Sohan Lal unpacked his food from his tiffin-carrier and hastily swallowed it in a corner; Mr Chaddha sat and read a book, swinging one leg and making notes in the margin; the other lecturers carried on a low-toned conversation about dearness allowances. Once Mr Khanna came down, addressed them all as 'Gentlemen' and disappeared again upstairs. The students thronged noisily in the corridor and out in the street, and Mrs Khanna's tea tasted of stale tea-leaves.

His mother waited eagerly for him at home. She cooked all the things she knew he liked, tidied his clothes and bought him a new bottle of hair-oil. As soon as he came home, she began to talk to him and never stopped. Even while he was having a bath, she talked to him through the bathroom door. Afterwards she made him lie down and rubbed his temples and forehead, though he had no headache. She rubbed and rubbed, looking complacent and happy as she did so. 'What is a mother for,' she said, 'if not to spoil her only son?' His eyes were shut and he felt profoundly gloomy. 'Ah, son,' she said and sighed, 'there is nothing like a mother's love.'

Prem felt this to be true. Nobody would ever love him again, he thought, like she did. Who else would serve him like this, fuss over him, cook his favourite dishes, massage his temples? It was perhaps what one expected of a wife – but all Indu did was go away with her uncle without even leaving a message for him. He felt tears filling into his eyes behind the closed lids and hastily turned his head away. 'No one can ever take the place of a mother,' said his mother.

He hoped to get a letter from Indu but nothing came. He found staying in the house had a very depressing effect on him, so in the evening he decided to go for a walk. On the way down he looked through the fly-screens of the Seigals' house and saw Mr Seigal at the card-table and, on the veranda, Mrs Seigal crocheting and having conversation with the wives of the other card players. They all looked so happy and comfortable that he quite forgot Mrs Seigal's tears which he had pitied a few days ago. Now he pitied only himself.

His life seemed a complete failure to him. In his present mood it even gave him a grim satisfaction to count up his various failures: he could not earn sufficient money; his career as a teacher was turning out to be unpromising; he had no real friend – even Raj, who had once been a real friend, had deserted him; he was not a successful husband. If he had thought further, he would probably have been able to find many more failures, but at this last one he stopped short and brooded about it. It was because he was not a successful husband that she had gone away; he had not been able to make her obedient and respectful; if she had been obedient and respectful, she would not have dared to go away. Or if she had liked him better, she would not have wanted to go away.

He had crossed the little children's park and had reached the bazaar. As usual at this time of the evening, a lot of shopping was going on. All the booths were lit up by electric light bulbs dangling from their wooden roofs. By the side of the road stood men with little barrows, illuminated by bright flares of naphtha light, selling cheap fruits or sugar-cane juice or coloured drinks in second-hand bottles. Prem thought why does she not like me enough to want to stay with me? He felt very much hurt. He had thought that perhaps she had begun to grow fond of him a little, but now he saw that this was not so. For the first time he thought about how he felt about her: yes, he thought, he had begun to grow fond of her.

Perhaps because he had grown used to her. He was used to her being there when he came home from the college and he was used to having her sleep next to him and used to her smell which was a mixture of hair-oil and perspiration and vanilla essence and a special woman-smell – used to so many things that he felt quite dizzy now when he thought about them all. He had not realized that there were so many. Yet she, it seemed, had not got used to him at all. If she had done so, she would have come back at once because she would not have been able to bear missing all the things she had got used to.

He came, with a pang, to a sweetmeat stall. She loved sweetmeats so much, yet only once had he brought some for her. He had promised to bring her more, had promised to bring some every day, yet he had not done so. He was selfish and mean, and she was right to go away from him. But now how he longed to buy sweetmeats for her!

He looked at the rows of yellow and green and white and pink and silvery chunks, with the flies hovering over them, and the proprietor, very large and fat with huge stomach and calves and many chins, sitting crosslegged above his goods and indolently waving his hand at the flies. Prem groped in his pocket to see how much money he had with him. But what was the use of buying now? He could neither send them to her nor keep them for her. He bitterly regretted all the opportunities of buying things for her he had wasted when she was still here. He remembered how once he had bought a little bag of nuts and raisins for himself and had quickly eaten it before he got home so that he would not have to give her any. Even that much, even a little bag of nuts and raisins costing a few annas, he had grudged her!

There were so many booths in the bazaar, so many things to buy as a present for Indu. Pots and pans and gleaming brass tumblers, coloured and gilded pictures of gods and saints, tiny bottles of scent essence and clay images and sticks of incense and bolts and bolts of cloth and fine thin saris printed with flowers suspended fluttering above the doorways. He again felt the money in his pocket and decided that he would buy something for her. Not sweetmeeats, but something that would keep. He did not have to think long; he knew at once that he wanted to buy her something that she could wear and be proud of; something shiny and beautiful. He would send it to her and she would remember him and perhaps be sorry that she had gone away without even leaving a message for him. Or he might keep it for her. Then he would be able to see the expression of pleasure on her face when he gave it to her; and she would know that he had been thinking of her while she was away.

He lingered outside a cloth stall and was beckoned in by the proprietor. There was a narrow little bench, and he perched himself on the very edge of it. Two fat middle-aged women, freshly bathed and puffed out in clean starched saris of white organdie, also sat on the bench with him; they looked sideways for a moment, giving him rather a contemptuous glance, then turned back, one to digging among the billows of materials which the shopman had already taken down for them, the other to range a commanding eye over the bolts of cloth stacked up to the ceiling. Prem sat shyly and with his hands pushed tight between his knees. His eyes too ranged over the materials, not so much out of curiosity as out of embarrassment. But at once he saw what he wanted: a shimmering pink satin. What a beautiful blouse it would make for her. He looked at it admiringly as it was brought down for him: how soft, how pink. It reminded him of Indu's tongue as he had seen it come flicking out to lick at sweetmeats.

He took his parcel, which was tied with newspaper and string, and walked home and stole into the bedroom with it. There he unpacked it, and he felt happy when he saw the pink material shine out at him. He stroked it and rubbed his cheek against it. How lovely it was! Surely she would like it? Very softly he pressed it against his mouth. Then his mother called, 'Son? Did you enjoy your walk, son?' He hid the material under the shirts in his drawer and went to sit with her in the sitting-room.

He often nowadays tried to think of excuses not to have to go home. Only there were not many other places he could go to. It made him feel very lonely to roam about by himself; and there was no friend to roam with him. Raj was busy with his office and his family; Sohan Lal had to cycle to Mehrauli; and that left only Hans. Perhaps Hans could be the friend he needed – the friend with whom he could spend pleasant social evenings, with whom he could have long dis- cussions, with whom he could share all his inward thoughts and prob- lems. He very much wanted such a friend.

One day he told his mother that he would be home late in the evening. 'Some urgent work,' he murmured. 'Go, child,' she sighed. 'I am here to see to everything.' This made him feel vaguely guilty and as if he were evading his duty. However, the feeling left him as soon as he left her, and by evening he went quite cheerfully to Hans' house.

'He's in his room, dear,' Kitty said. She was sitting writing in a little notebook, a pair of very large spectacles perched on the tip of her nose. She only glanced briefly at Prem over the top of these spectacles, then licked the point of the tiny stub of pencil she held and carried on writing. She looked very much intent, so Prem did not like to disturb her further but tiptoed quietly past her and out at an opposite door. This led him into the courtyard, which was paved with marble tiles and must have been a very handsome courtyard once. But now it had some not too clean washing strung across it, and there were two rick- ety and sagging string-cots, a ladder with four rungs missing propped against a wall and a mangy parrot in a bent wire cage. Mohammed Ali was squatting on the threshold of the kitchen. He looked mel- ancholy and even rather depressed, as if he were thinking of better times. Prem's intrusion seemed to annoy him, and when asked to point out Hans' room, he did so very ungraciously.

It was the untidiest room Prem had ever seen. Books, papers, boots, pieces of clothing, empty cups were scattered all over. Hans sat on the floor with his legs crossed under him and his hands laid palm upwards on his knees; there was a rather self-conscious look of meditation on his face. Prem thought Hans might be embarrassed by the disorder in the room, so he said quickly, 'How nice your room is'; but after he had said it, he thought perhaps that was wrong, because it drew attention to the room. He covered it up quickly with, 'It was very hot today.'

'Today I achieve nothing,' Hans said from the floor. He pounded his fist against his forehead in a mood of anguish 'My thoughts are wild and bad, I cannot control them.'

Prem's heart leapt, partly with shock, partly with excitement. Did Hans too have these moments of shame that he himself had when he thought unworthy thoughts about Indu and could not stop thinking them? He sat down rather breathlessly and wondered whether it would be possible to have an intimate talk about Hans. 'I try to gather them in one point' – Hans cupped his hand – 'but – pfutsch! – they scatter wild like this – ' and he flung out both his arms as if he were chasing away birds. 'Do you also suffer like this?'

'Yes, I – ' Prem slid down from the chair, which he had originally chosen, to sit with Hans on the floor. He wanted to be near him, so that they could talk in low voices. 'Sometimes I feel great shame at my thoughts.'

'You are right – one must feel shame when one fails!' Hans shouted very loudly, which made Prem nervous that they might be overheard. 'Why must our thoughts be full with trivial things, when Reality is there waiting for us to grasp her with both the hands?' He got up to stride around the room, impatiently kicking aside a pair of braces as he did so. Apparently he was not at all embarrassed at the disorder in his room; nor by his appearance, though all he was wearing was a very short pair of shorts.

'The sadhus are right,' Hans said. 'One must sit on nails and mortify the flesh.' He pulled viciously at the flesh around his midriff, shouting, 'It must be mortified so the thoughts will be controlled!'

Prem hung his head. Perhaps Hans was right; perhaps he had been too soft with himself, indulging his unworthy thoughts instead of plucking them out. He felt a desire to confess to Hans. If only Hans would sit down close to him: he could not very well shout about his confession.

But Hans was still walking around the room in agitation, so at last Prem said shyly from the floor, 'I am also suffering from this same difficulty.'

Hans stopped pacing, and he squatted down on his haunches in front of Prem. He scanned Prem's face.

'Yes, I – you see,' but now that it came to confessing, Prem did not know how to.

'That is interesting, very interesting,' Hans said, his eyes still roaming Prem's face as if he wanted to read secrets there.

Prem looked down and drew invisible patterns on the floor. He wanted to tell Hans, but found it unbearably difficult to do so.

'Your mind is also fixed too much on the things of the world?'

Prem nodded silently. He swallowed, wanting to define what things they were specifically fixed on, but instead of speaking he cleared his throat. Telling of these things would involve mentioning, or at least referring to, the existence of Indu; and he could not bring himself to that.

'But for you, an Indian, how easy it is!' Hans cried. 'By nature you are unworldly. But my nature is so that I thrust outwards to adventure and action – '

'I am weak,' Prem murmured, sinking his head lower and lower while he continued furiously to draw imaginary patterns.

'A Westerner's nature is so that he feels he must conquer the world. Can I change my nature so that I can conquer myself? This is what I strive for.'

'I have not been married very long,' Prem said in what was hardly more than a whisper. 'Perhaps that is why – ' but he could not say it further. He tried to force himself. It is my duty to tell, he persuaded himself; he is my friend. 'I believe very much in friendship,' he said. Hans looked at him attentively, as if he hoped to hear something very wise and true. 'Friends must share everything. They must not hide anything from each other. Even if they don't like to tell something to their friend, still they must tell it.' Hans continued to look at him with that same expression of attentiveness, his pale eyes eager for knowledge. 'For instance,' Prem said, 'I am your friend. But what do you know of me? Only by looking at my face you can learn nothing. If I want you to know me, I must open my heart to you and let you read everything that is there – '

'I understand you!' Hans cried. 'Maya! Illusion! You are saying the outward thing, the face, is Illusion, speak!' He grasped Prem's hands and squeezed them. Admiration shone from his face. Prem, allowing his hands to be squeezed, thought it better not to say anything further. He was embarrassed and also disappointed, but he did not wish to destroy the good impression he had apparently created.

There was still no letter from Indu. Every day he looked for one and every day he was disappointed. He left for the college in the morning with this feeling of disappointment, but returned at lunchtime buoyant with hope because the midday post might have brought a letter. Then he was disappointed again; and in the evening the process was repeated.

Sometimes he got angry and wanted to write her an angry letter. Once he did actually write such a letter. He had set his class a Hindi poem to paraphrase into prose; and while they were busy with this, he took a piece of paper and began to write to Indu. His students shuffled in their seats, sucked their pens and appealed to one another for help. Mr Chaddha marched up and down in front of his blackboard, with his hands behind his back, lecturing in an important voice on the origins and development of the Congress movement. Prem thought only of his letter. He frowned as he wrote: 'What harm did I do that you had to run from me without leaving even one note for me, and also no letter have you sent for me? Do I drink spirits or I beat you or perhaps I do not give you sufficient money for your household that you must treat me like this?' The more he wrote the angrier he became. There was perspiration on his forehead and he was biting his lip. He did not notice that his students had finished or had given up and had gathered into groups to play four-on-ace. 'It is the wife's duty to stay with her husband, when once she has been married to him then she must stay with him and not run home to her parents when this whim comes over her.' It was only when the bell rang to mark the end of the lesson that he remembered his class. He gathered in the exercise they had done, and spoke to them with a severity which was calculated to make up for his previous neglect. His letter he had folded tightly and thrust into his pocket. He did not tell himself that he did not mean to post it, but on his way home he tore it into very small pieces and threw it into the sewage canal.

He spent as much time as his mother would let him lying on the big bed in his bedroom. He looked at the two cupids with their arms and wings entwined at the head of the bed and felt great longing and loneliness. How he had loved this bed, this room. But now it had lost everything; he sniffed the air, but instead of the smell of perspiration, hair-oil and vanilla essence there was only the the smell of the disinfectant soap with which his mother had had the floor washed. He opened the drawer and took out the piece of pink satin he had bought, and he stroked it and admired it and put his lips to it. Then he went back to lie on the bed and looked with melancholy eyes at the cupids. Soon his mother would be calling him – 'Son? What are you doing, son?' – and he would have to go and sit with her in the living-room and listen to her talk about Ankhpur and her sons-in-law and the new Principal. And about the servant-boy. Every day she said, 'He must be told to go.' Every day Prem promised to dismiss him. Yet he never did.

He had always been rather put out by the boy's indifferent, indeed almost contemptuous, attitude towards himself, and there had been a time when he would have dearly liked to get rid of him. But lately – in fact, ever since Indu's departure – he felt that the boy had softened towards him. Not that they ever spoke together or that the boy put himself out to serve Prem. But somehow he made it clear that he no longer regarded Prem as an enemy; and he even managed to suggest that they were allies. Allies against whom and in what common cause Prem did not wish to think. But he did nothing to contradict the tacit suggestion. Thus, when Prem's mother began to scold in the kitchen, the boy would usually come into the room where Prem was sitting and pretend to have some work to do there. He never appealed to Prem for support, indeed he never as much as looked at him; he had his back to him and made idle dusting gestures or rubbed at a stain on the wall. Prem in return pretended not to notice that he was there. It was only when his mother followed from the kitchen and began to abuse the boy in front of Prem, that Prem made a show of joining in the scolding. But he felt that the boy understood that he had to do it, for appearance sake.

His days seemed very dull to Prem. He could get no interest out of the college – everything there was every day so very much the same. He no longer felt even the stirrings of ambition. There seemed no point in being a good teacher in a college where the students were only interested in getting into another, better college. Teaching was a job that had to be got through from eight to five every day in order to enable one to collect a salary on the third of every month. That was the way Sohan Lal and most of the other teachers looked at it. Perhaps they too had started off with high ideals the way he had;

maybe they even still held them; but it was, he recognized, impossible to reconcile such ideals with the reality of Khanna Private College.

He thought, vaguely, of looking for another job, in some finer better college where ideals were high and students looked up to their teachers and respected and even revered them, and the teachers loved their students and strove to mould them to the best principles, and the Principal was concerned not with profit but with an ideal of service to youth. But for one thing he did not know where to find such a college, and for another he doubted whether he would be accepted there. He was lucky to have even got into Khanna Private College, for he had only a second-class B.A. and no teaching experience: he knew it was the influence of his father's friends that had placed him here, and perhaps Mr Khanna's willingness to be satisfied with less than others since the salaries he paid out were also less than those of others.

The question of salary irked Prem less than it had been doing up till now. He even felt too listless to think about it much. And what was the use of thinking about an increase in salary? With Indu away, it was almost as if he had no wife; and with her away, he found it impossible to take the coming of a baby seriously. So the burden of supporting a family, the thought of which had so oppressed him, had lifted from him. But now he missed it. Now that it was gone from him, he craved again for the sensation of being a family man with duties and responsibilities. He thought almost enviously of Raj, who had a wife and daughter to look after, and was frowning and anxious with worrying about how to get the lavatory repaired or pay the school fees in the coming years when his child would have to start going to school. At least with such burdens one was someone – a family man, a member of society, living next to, in rows and colonies with, other such members of society who had the same worries. But Prem – what was he? He was no longer a student living in his father's house: he had lost interest in his mother and in her cooking and in talk of Ankhpur. But what was he instead? Where did he belong? It seemed to him now that he belonged nowhere, was nothing, was nobody.

He became daily more depressed, and it was in this mood that he decided to go and visit the swami again. He was not sure quite what it was he wanted or hoped from the swami, but he felt a quite urgent desire to visit him. He did not tell Sohan Lal of this desire, but went quietly, almost furtively, by himself. He thought he knew exactly where the house was, but when he got into the main bazaar, he found he had forgotten which side street it was they had taken. He tried several, but they all turned out to be the wrong ones. It was confusing, for in each of these narrow alleys were the same cloth stalls Prem had remembered from his first visit, with it seemed the same sleek merchants in fine white muslin clothes sitting on mats inside them, smoking hookahs or writing in large ledgers or only staring out with uninterested eyes. The stalls were all large and prosperous and as calm and peaceful as a drawing-room. But though Prem thought every time that this surely was the one, he could never find the archway leading to the courtyard of the swami's house. There were other doorways and he hopefully went through them, only to find himself once in the precincts of a disused mosque, another time in a large carpenter's workshop, a third time in a nest of squatters who had settled down in the niches of an old house and cluttered up the courtyard with their cooking-fires, their washing, with their battered tins, their useless stubble-chinned old men and hordes of children.

But at last he found it. He passed through one arched and fretted old doorway and then through another, and there he was in the courtyard where the cobbler sat under a tree hammering nails into a shoe. Prem walked up the narrow staircase. Now that he had actually got here, he felt shy. He did not know whether the swami would remember him and, if he did remember him, whether he would not reproach him for having stayed away so long. He wished he had come with Sohan Lal, and he could not understand now why he had felt the need to come thus secretly by himself.

The low arched door which led to the swami's room stood open. Prem peeped in and saw that the room was empty. A few mats lay askew on the floor and there were some flower petals scattered about and trailed across the swami's bed lay a piece of orange-coloured cloth. The room was sweet and heavy with incense, and a little wisp of smoke still came from the last smouldering remains of joss-stick which had been stuck into the window-frame. Altogether the room had an air of only just having been abandoned by a crowd of lively people, though apart from the bed and the mats and a little oblong grey tin trunk under the bed, it was quite empty. Prem climbed farther up the stairs. He was sure they must all be somewhere, so he was not surprised when the last landing brought him on to the roof and there they were.

But what did surprise him was the roof itself, which had been made into a charming garden. The parapet was covered with clusters of red creepers, and there were flowers in pots all round and a little leafy bower under which stood a garlanded image of Vishnu. There was even a tiny ornamental pond built up on stones, with water crystal-clear and many-coloured fish swimming around. The swami in his orange robe was walking up and down the flagged paving with a young man on each side of him and his arms slung around their shoulders. Other young men stood round in groups. It was sunset time, and the sky, which looked very near, had such a strong glow that everything seemed tinted with an orange colour which was just like that of the swami's robe.

The swami recognized Prem at once and said, while Prem was respectfully touching his feet, 'How do you like our garden?'

'It is so beautiful,' Prem said eagerly.

'Yes,' said the swami, and he smiled all round as if he were seeing for the first time how beautiful it was.

A tall handsome young man with a very dark skin and a frown on his face, said impatiently, 'What need have we of these things?'

The swami turned his smiling face on him: 'Why not? It is always nice to see how God sports with flowers and fish and birds in his playful mood.'

'God's place is in my heart,' said the young man severely. 'What do I care for anything outside of that?'

'God has many attributes!' called one young man in a challenging tone.

The dark young man turned on him: 'God has no attributes! He is without shape or Form.'

'Now we have started,' said another youth in mock despair.

The swami said, 'But I only want our friend here to enjoy our garden'; and he smiled at Prem, who answered, 'Oh I enjoy it very much.'

'What else matters?' said the swami. He turned to the frowning young man and lightly touched his cheek with his finger-tips: 'Don't be angry with me,' he said in a pleading voice. 'For some God has attributes, for others He has none, and discussion on this topic can be sharp and everlasting. But in the end all that matters is that we should love Him and enjoy His love.'

'How true!' Prem cried with pleasure. It was not a problem he had ever really considered, but now that he heard it stated like this, he at once gave it his enthusiastic assent.

But the angry young man said, 'You make everything too simple.'

The swami smilingly bowed his head. He looked ready and even glad to listen to a rebuke, like a father proud to have his opinion corrected by a beloved son. 'If you make it too simple,' the young man said, 'fools will come and sit with gaping mouths, and then afterwards they will set themselves up as teachers and astonish other fools with foolery.'

'There was once a village headman,' the swami said. Prem moved in closer, so as not to lose a word; his eyes were fixed on the swami's face and there was an expectant smile on his lips. The other young men also drew close, some with their arms clasped round each other's neck. Someone leant his elbow in a carelessly friendly manner on Prem's shoulder. Prem felt proud and happy and stood quite still under the weight of this friendly elbow. 'It was the time of his son's marriage. He had made a very good match for him with the daughter of a rich man in another village. He was very proud of this match, so much so that when the time came to make preparations for the feasting, he did not consider his friends and relatives good enough to be invited. In the end he invited only the three richest men in his village. But it so happened that on the day they were to set off for the bride's village, all these three sent excuses to say they could not come. So the village headman had to arrive alone with his son, without relatives or friends or supporters. What shame he felt then before the bride's family!'

The angry young man curled his lips and threw back his head; he looked very proud: 'God shall never want friends,' he said, and his voice too was full of pride.

At that moment the temple bells began to ring, and there was chanting and clashing of cymbals in the temples in the city below. 'You are right,' the swami said, tenderly looking at the angry young man.

'No,' said this young man, 'that is not what I meant. God does not need temples or priests or bells.'

'He needs love and a pure heart,' the swami said. His eyes were now very large and brilliant and his lips were parted in a smile. Then he was singing in ecstasy. He sang 'O God, let me drink you like wine!' Soon others had joined in. They were singing and dancing and clapping their hands in joy. The swami turned round and round in a circle, laughing like a child. The angry young man was on his knees, watching him, and from time to time he threw back his head and gave a burst of happy laughter. Someone had begun to play on a flute, and this music too ascended on spirals of joy. Prem stood by and watched.

There was great longing, almost like pain, in his heart. He wanted to join in the dancing, but his limbs felt heavy and fettered. He thought that if he could shake off these fetters, then the longing in his heart too would resolve and he would be free to sing and dance and be happy with the others. His eyes filled with tears when he thought of this, and he trembled with the expectation of happiness.

Indu wrote 'How are you? I am well. We are all well. Please do not worry at all.' Her handwriting was like that of a child. Prem read the letter several times, and his mother put on her spectacles and scrutinized it with pursed lips. The servant-boy hovered round, anxious for someone to read it out to him. In the end he asked Prem, 'What does she write?' 'Is there no work for you in the kitchen?' Prem's mother shouted. The servant-boy disappeared. After some time Prem followed him into the kitchen and said, 'She says she is well and not to worry.'

He left for college in quite a lighthearted mood. He was not at all embarrassed by the students lounging outside the college and he got through his classes without any difficulty. Afterwards he sat with Sohan Lal in the staff-room, drinking Mrs Khanna's tea and feeling more contented than he had been since Indu's departure. He told Sohan Lal 'Today I had a letter from my wife who has gone to stay with her parents'; he said this in a matter-of-fact tone, as if it were an everyday occurrence for him to get a letter from his wife, and indeed a quite ordinary and accepted fact that she should go and stay with her parents. 'She says she is well,' he added. Sohan Lal sat by sympathetically; he looked ready to listen to a lot more. Prem would like to have told him a lot more, but there was nothing he could put into words. So instead he said, 'Yesterday I went there.'

An expression of eagerness came on Sohan Lal's face. 'Really?' he said. 'What did he say?'

'He talked about – oh, many things.'

'He sang? He said the name of God?'

'Yes.'

'Ah,' said Sohan Lal with a smile of longing. After a while he said, 'Who else was there?'

Prem told him about the angry young man. 'That is Vishvanathan,' Sohan Lal said. 'Swamiji loves him very much for he knows that Vishvanathan thinks about God so much that he has cut all his ties with the world.'

Prem sighed with admiration. He thought of tall, black Vishvanathan, fierce with love for God, careless and contemptuous of the worldly things other men longed for. 'How wonderful to see a young man give up everything for God,' he said with shining eyes.

But Sohan Lal looked despondent; and when he spoke it was almost bitterly: 'What is there so much to give up? Who would not turn to God and take pleasure only in thinking about Him, if he could?' Prem was surprised by the other's tone, which sounded resentful. 'It is easy for a young man whose marriage has not been made to vow himself to God,' Sohan Lal said. 'What burdens has he, what responsibilities? He is free to do as he pleases.' Prem nodded in agreement. He was rather embarrassed by Sohan Lal's outburst, which was too unexpected for him to decide how to react to it.

'Here in our India,' said Sohan Lal, 'it is so that while we are still children and know nothing of what we want, they take us and tie us up with a wife and children.'

'True,' said Prem, nodding sagely.

'So that when we are old enough to know what the world is and what God is, then it is too late, for we have a burden on our back which we cannot shake off for the rest of our days.'

Prem tried to look wise; but he did not feel particularly stirred by Sohan Lal's words. He could not help admitting to himself that he rather liked his burden, which was Indu. He thought of her letter with the child's handwriting and felt like smiling to himself.

He soon returned to thoughts of how to support his family. He lay on his bed at home, under the two cupids, and frowned with anxiety. But the anxiety was deliberate and he enjoyed it. It made him feel responsible. He thought about asking Mr Khanna for a rise in salary and about asking Mr Seigal for a reduction in rent. He told himself that both these tasks must be achieved before Indu returned. Then he got up and opened the drawer and took out the piece of pink satin. He folded and refolded it to feel its softness. She would sit on the floor and sew it into a blouse for herself; and on special occasions – on occasions when she wore her jewellery and her platform-sole shoes and jasmine in her hair – she would put it on and it would fit tight and gleaming over her breasts. He smiled to himself and shut the drawer. Then he got back to serious thoughts.

After a while he came out into the sitting-room and found his mother sitting on her bed, telling her beads and saying God's name. In between she sighed. Prem knew at once that she was thinking more of her own troubles than of God. It had always been like that: prayer stimulated her to dwell on the circumstances of her own life and to regret them. Even on happy occasions, such as a wedding or name-giving ceremony or some other festival when prayers were said, she always reverted to feeling sorry for herself.

Prem distinctly remembered one Diwali, when he was about five years old. They had all gathered in the little prayer-room, he and his father and his mother and his four sisters and an old aunt of his father's who had been staying with them at the time. His mother and the old aunt were lighting the little lights in front of the garlanded image of the goddess Lakshmi, offering rice and sweetmeats and in-toning their prayers. The aunt was still chanting lustily, when Prem's mother suddenly clasped her hands before her face and began to sob loudly. Prem was shocked and looked from one person to the other for guidance. His sisters sat straight-backed and stared at the goddess and did not dare move. His father was wiping his forehead with a handkerchief as if he were feeling hot from the burning lights; his face had assumed that pompous look it always had when he was embarrassed. The aunt continued the prayers on her own, and when she had finished, she distributed the sweetmeats among them all. Prem's mother also took one and as she put it in her mouth, she wailed, 'What is my life? What has become of me?' Prem's father wiped his forehead harder and cleared his throat. The four daughters still stared at the goddess; only their jaws moved as they chewed the sweetmeats. 'Once I was a child in my parents' house,' Prem's mother sobbed. 'I was as free of worries as this child here,' and she clasped Prem's head which he jerked away, for he was rather nervous of her in this mood. 'Now what has become of me?' she cried. No one answered. There was no answer, for everyone knew that she was perfectly contented and even proud to be the wife of a Principal and in charge of a household of her own. And after the prayers were over, she herself seemed to forget her outburst. At any rate, she behaved much as usual and came with them to see the Diwali lights in the town, sitting in the horse-carriage Prem's father had hired for the occasion and apparently enjoying the outing.

After that Prem became used to her bursting into tears in the course of her prayers – indeed, he even expected it. Consequently he was not at all surprised when he heard her deep sigh as she sat on the bed and told her beads; soon she had dropped the rosary into her lap and was wiping tears from her eyes and her cheeks with the end of her sari. 'What has become of my life?' she sobbed.

But even though he had expected her tears, Prem could not help feeling sorry for her when he actually saw them. He cleared his throat, ran his hand over his hair and wished he could say something to comfort her.

'What am I today?' his mother said. 'No one cares for me, no one thinks of me, I am nothing, less than nothing.'

'We all care for you,' Prem said hoarsely.

His mother covered her face with her sari and sobbed from behind it. 'Would it not be better for me to be dead?'

'Why do you speak like that?' Prem mumbled. He hardly dared look at her. Though he had never shown any disrespect towards her, yet he knew he was guilty. He did not need her or want her any more the way he had done before he was married.

'Why should you care for me? You have your wife now, soon you will have a family – what is your mother to you now?' She wiped at her eyes again. 'It is so in life. When we are old we are forgotten. No one has heard of us any more.'

'Yesterday I brought a present for you,' Prem said. 'I wanted it to be a surprise for you.' He went into the bedroom, opened the drawer and took out the piece of pink satin.

Her eyes lit up as soon as she saw it. 'You brought this for me?' She stroked it, held it up to the light, touched it against her cheek. 'What is the use of bringing such a thing for an old woman like me?' She held it in front of herself. 'For your wife you should bring.'

'I brought it for you.'

One evening he decided he wanted to see Raj again. He felt Raj was now the person with whom he had most in common and he wanted to have a long discussion with him about the problems of family life.

Raj's office was a sub-division of the Ministry of Food. It was housed in a row or barracks, consisting of one room next to the other and with a long narrow veranda running all down the row. The doors and windows were boarded with screens made of scented grass on which water was to be sprinkled to keep the rooms cool; however, the grass was quite dry and the rooms looked hot. Each room was divided into cubicles and they were all crowded with regulation office chairs, steel filing cabinets, tables littered over with odd charts and papers and brimming wire trays, telephones and big old-fashioned typewriters. Among these sat many clerks with their sleeves rolled up high and their foreheads wet with perspiration; from time to time they drank water or wiped their palms with handkerchiefs. The rooms looked close and tense with heat; old fans in inadequate working order creaked slow and lazy from the ceiling, stirring up hot air.

Prem wandered down the stretch of veranda, peering round each grass-screened door to see if he could find Raj. But though all the clerks were rather like Raj, with oiled hair and thin worried faces, none of them actually was he. Prem wondered whether he could ask someone. He hardly dared, for everybody looked hot and bad-tempered; and after one short impatient glance when he first peered in, they took no further notice of him. The peons, who stood lounging outside on the veranda in their khaki uniforms, also took no notice of him; they were either sleeping or carrying on desultory conversation with one another.

Prem lingered on the veranda and felt excluded. All these men were Government servants, graded correctly according to their official standing, with salaries and increments laid down precisely, with so many days sick leave a year, with a dearness allowance and family allowance apportioned to them. They belonged here, among the regulation chairs and tables and grass screens; they had their allotted share in the working of files and ordinances, and when they retired, they were given a pension which was in a fixed and settled ration to what they had been earning all their working lives.

Prem wanted very much to be one of them. If one succeeded in getting into government service, one's future was settled; there was nothing more to fear. And one belonged somewhere, one was part of something bigger than oneself. That was just what Prem wanted: he felt a great need to be absorbed. He knew that this could never happen to him in Khanna Private College, for Khanna Private College was neither big nor impartial enough. But Government was: it was like a stern kind father who supported his children and demanded nothing in return but their subservience.

At exactly five there was a rush from out of all the office rooms. Youngish men in frequently washed white shirts and thin gaberdine trousers rushed to the bus-stops or to the close-packed cycle sheds. Some of them already wore their cycle-clips round their legs. Prem was afraid of missing Raj in this crowd of clerks who all resembled him so closely, but it was not long before he saw him, hurrying with the same frowning intensity as the others towards the bus-stop. He was not at all pleased to see Prem. 'Why do you come here?' was his first greeting, and Prem at once felt guilty.'

'This is a Government office,' Raj said severely. 'It does not look nice for people who are not Government servants to come and pay social visits.'

'I was only waiting outside,' Prem mumbled. But he knew this was no excuse.

He walked down the road with Raj. After a while he said, 'Do you think it is possible for me to get into Government service?' and he looked anxiously at Raj's stern profile.

Raj pursed his lips. 'It is not easy.'

'I know.'

'To make an application one has to fill in a long form and then there is a competitive examination and also an interview.'

'An examination?' Prem asked tremulously. He thought he had already passed all the examinations it was his duty in life to pass, and he did not feel like starting again.

'A competitive examination,' Raj said with some relish. 'It is very difficult.'

Prem hung his head. 'I only wanted to – '

'I know,' Raj said dryly. 'There are many people like you who only want to get into Government service.'

'No, there is something else also,' Prem said. But he found it difficult to explain what this was. The fact that he wanted to belong somewhere; and not only that, but also his whole position as house-holder, as husband, which he wanted to stabilize, register as it were, make sure and accepted. He was so different from the Prem who had been a student in Ankhpur College and had lived in his father's house. He did not know how to say all this to Raj, so instead he said, 'One day please bring your family to my house, I invite you.'

'The bus fare to your house will come very expensive for me,' Raj said.

'When my wife comes home. She has gone to her parents.'

Raj gently shook his head and made clicking noises with his tongue.'

'What is the matter?'

Raj went on shaking his head: 'Why did you let her go?'

Prem was embarrassed. He could not admit that she had gone on her own, without waiting for his consent, and indeed without even as much as leaving a note for him. But he was afraid that Raj might guess at something like that, so he said as lightly as he could, 'Why not? They are her parents.'

Raj looked shrewd: 'Did you have a quarrel?'

'Of course not,' Prem said, kicking at stones on the road.

'That is when wives usually go home to their parents. Is your mother still staying with you?'

'Yes,' Prem said, kicking away.

'Ah,' Raj said in a triumphant I-guessed-as-much voice.

'They lived very well together,' Prem said unconvincingly.

Raj gave a mirthless laugh: 'There is not much you can teach me about these things. Please remember, I have been married a good deal longer than you have. Here is my bus-stop. Good-bye.'

'One minute,' Prem said. He felt that they had just reached to the kind of conversation he had been longing to have for a long time. But Raj saw his bus coming and he broke off into a run to join the queue at the bus-stop. Prem ran with him, shouting 'When can we meet again?' as he ran.

Raj came too late. He was pushed back by the other passengers and the bus left without him. 'How rude some people are in their behaviour,' he said indignantly.

'Perhaps we can meet again in the Regal Cinema at our usual time?'

'Like college boys you want us to meet in a cinema,' Raj said.

'I will take you to a new place which I have found where we will get very good pakoras.' Prem looked at him pleadingly.

Just then another bus came. Raj quickly elbowed his way to the door, but when he had got on, he called to Prem, 'I will see you on Monday.'

But Monday seemed a long way off, and Prem felt heavy with the longing to talk about his life. And because there was no one he could talk to, he sat on the bed with his legs tucked under him and a note-pad on his lap. He wrote a letter to Indu: 'If you will come home now, I shall be glad.' He was almost tempted to write that he missed her, but he felt shy. For one thing, it was not something he felt it was proper for a husband to tell his wife; and for another, he knew all her family would read the letter and, if he wrote anything very personal like that, they would laugh or perhaps even be shocked. So he wrote, 'We are all well. It is not very hot yet here for this time of year. There is a very good crop of mangoes and they have come down to only

102

twelve annas a seer.' He sucked his pen a little and stared at the two cupids entwined so lovingly at the head of the bed. And then he looked at the little table with the gilded lion-feet on which she had kept her hair-oil and her glass phial of scent; and he sniffed the air and smelt the carbolic soap which had replaced the small of perspiration, vanilla essence and hair-oil.

Suddenly he was writing quite differently, and instead of dawdling and hesitating over each word, his pen raced over the paper: 'Why did you go away from me? I long for you and sometimes I feel like crying with tears because you are not there. I think of you so often. The house is empty without you and my heart also is empty. In the night I lie alone in our bed. Then I want to feel you and I remember how warm you always are and so soft like silk. I want to stroke you and kiss you everywhere with my mouth and then I want to be inside you. When I think of this, I feel I shall die with longing so much for you.'

'Son!' His mother came into the room. 'What are you doing, son?' Prem quickly covered the writing with his hand.

'You are writing a letter? You are writing to your wife? Let me see.' She held out her hand.

'No no,' he said. He tore off the sheet and crumpled it almost viciously and held it tight in his fist. He felt hot with shame. 'I am only – '

'I have cooked rice and mincemeat for you, son,' she said proudly. 'Come and eat.'

'I am just coming. Please take it out for me.' When she had gone, he released the crumpled ball of paper from his fist and let it drop to the floor. He took matches and set fire to it on the stone floor; he swept up the ashes carefully in his hand and threw them out of the window. He felt terribly ashamed of himself. Hans is right, he thought; a person like me, with so many evil uncontrolled thoughts, must mortify the flesh until all shameful desire is purged away. And yet, even while he was thinking this, he longed for Indu and to do to her all the things he had written.

After the tea-party had, from his point of view, proved such a failure, he had not liked to give much thought to his obligation to ask for a rise in salary. But it still remained, he knew, an obligation. Sooner or later he would have to approach Mr Khanna again on the subject. He was very reluctant to do so. He was put off by the thought of again going upstairs into Mr Khanna's living-room and standing there, asking for a rise in salary, while Mr Khanna ate his breakfast and Mrs Khanna looked suspiciously at Prem's feet lest they dirtied her carpet. He felt it was difficult to keep up one's dignity in such a situation.

But he could send a letter. It would be so much easier to state his case in writing, pointing out how he was a family man and had to pay 45 rupees rent a month. 'If I write a letter,' he told Sohan Lal, with whom he consulted on this point, 'I will be able to give my story at length and convince him it is really necessary for me to have a rise in salary.'

'You can try if you like,' said Sohan Lal in a voice which did not commit him to any comment on the success or unsuccess of the venture.

So in the evening, when he got home, Prem tried. He sat down on the bed with a note-pad (the same on which he had begun to write his letter to Indu) and tried to formulate a petition to Mr Khanna. Since it was a petition he started off with 'If it please you, sir'; but after that it was difficult for him to progress. There were so many points to be considered. As he put it to Sohan Lal the next day: 'I will have to write in official style to make him see that my demand is just, but I also want to be personal and touching, so that his feelings will be softened.' It took several consultations more and a lot of sitting on the bed with the note-pad before he finally got his petition completed. He liked his beginning, which was straightforward and factual: 'I am a lecturer in your college.' From there he went on to define the duties of a lecturer, ending up with, 'and so, is it not right to presume that a lecturer's great responsibility to Youth and Learning entitles him to higher salary than is given to him?' After that he became official again ('I submit hereby my request for rise in salary') but followed it up with an account of his personal history. From then on he hinted rather than stated directly, 'You also must have learnt from experience, sir, that when once a man marries, soon other things follow and it is not long before he has the burden of a family to support', and ended up in a crescendo of personal appeal: 'I stand before you with folded hands and trust in your goodness that you will not turn aside the appeal of one who has only recently started out in life and is in need of assistance and kind thoughts from his elders.' After reading this over several times, he added 'and betters'.

There remained the problem of how to present this petition to Mr Khanna. He thought about it all evening. He saw himself knocking on

Mr Khanna's door, walking into the room with sure and certain steps, laying his letter before the Principal, joining his hands in a respectful manner, and then leaving the room as softly, courteously but confidently, as he had entered it. It seemed easy enough when he thought about it like that, but all the same he wished he did not have to do it. So much did he wish this, that he even looked in the morning's paper to see if there was no suitable job advertised for him. There was not, so he went to look in the old papers stacked on a shelf in the kitchen. And as he sat on the floor, looking through the columns of old papers, he remembered that other time when he had sat among the old papers on the kitchen floor looking for a possible job. He remembered that he had felt sad then; and he felt rather sad now. But it was different. The only thing that was the same was that there were no jobs advertised for him. He looked through column after column and wished he were an engineer or a town planner or a doctor. His mother called from inside, 'Son, why are you in the kitchen?' At that moment it occurred to him why it was so different from the other time he had looked through the papers for a job. Then he had felt sad because Indu was there; now he felt sad because she was not there. He folded the papers back and called to his mother that he was coming.

He did not shrink from his decision. Next day he really walked up the stairs to Mr Khanna's private apartment, holding the letter tightly in his hand. But his plan was upset when he saw that Mr Khanna was not there. Only Mrs Khanna and three other ladies. They sat in a close circle, each one stirring in a tea-cup; one lady was talking and the other leaning eagerly towards her. Their eyes were gleaming. 'Every afternoon from two to five when her husband was in office,' the lady was saying. The others swayed their heads and clicked their tongues. They did not notice Prem. 'And the children in the house all the time,' the lady said in a shocked gloating voice. 'Hai-hai,' said Mrs Khanna with another click of the tongue. The teaspoons went round in the cups in quick agitation.

Prem cleared his throat and the four heads spun round towards him. 'What do you want?' Mrs Khanna shouted hoarsely.

'Mr Khanna,' Prem said, holding out the letter. It shook slightly for his hand was trembling. The four ladies looked at him angrily.

'This is what it is like in a college,' Mrs Khanna told the others. 'Not one moment's rest or peace. Every minute these people come to bother you.'

'It is not right,' said one lady.

'They must be told,' said another.

'What is the use of telling,' said Mrs Khanna. 'Now leave your letter and go!' she shouted at Prem. They drew their chairs closer together and leant towards each other. 'And what is worse . . .' the lady began again. Prem shut the door behind him. As he walked down the stairs, he could hear a loud delighted gasp of shock emitted in chorus.

'It was very embarrassing for me,' Prem commented when he had told Sohan Lal about this occurrence. He could still feel the ladies' angry looks on his face. 'I am a lecturer of the college. I have the right to go upstairs.'

'She doesn't like us to come up,' Sohan Lal said in a matter-of-fact way.

'Why?' Prem insisted, ready to argue the point out. But Sohan Lal was not. He knew he could not afford to annoy the Principal's wife and that was all the argument needed for him.

'And who knows if she will give my letter,' Prem said in a despairing voice. The whole venture seemed to have failed. Not only had he been an object of anger and contempt to a group of ladies, but he had also delivered his petition into unsafe hands. He returned home in a highly unsatisfied state of mind.

3

The servant-boy stood out on the landing with a wide grin on his face: 'She is home,' he said. Prem walked past him and went straight into the bedroom. On the little table with gilded lion-feet stood a bottle of hair-oil, a comb, a little round tin of mascara and a glass phial of scent. Indu had her back to the door; she was hanging up her picture of Mother and Baby, stepping back several times to see if it was straight. Prem rubbed his hand against the side of his leg. His face was stern and strained, and he did not know what to say. Indu turned round and saw him, and she lowered her eyes and also did not know what to say. They stood like that for a while. At last Prem said, 'You have hung up your picture.' Indu nodded. 'It looks nice,' Prem said. His voice was hoarse; he was still rubbing his hand up and down against his trouser-leg.

'Son!'

'Your mother is calling,' Indu said in almost a whisper.

'Did you have a good journey?'

'It was very hot in the train.'

'I see,' Prem said, and they stood and did not say anything more.

'Son!'

'There were many people in your compartment?'

'She is calling you.'

'It is safer to travel in a compartment with many people, but sometimes there is great inconvenience.'

'It was very hot.'

'It has been very hot the whole week,' Prem said. 'I think next week it will be even hotter.' She really looked pregnant now, he noticed. Her figure protruded from the waist and she held herself balanced slightly backward. She seemed to him so beautiful that he was shy and fearful to look at her.

'Why don't you come when I call you?' said his mother. She stood between them, looking cross.

'I did not hear you,' Prem said.

'Come and have your tea, son. I have made for you.'

Indu stayed behind in the bedroom. Prem's mother stirred his tea for him: 'I have put a lot of sugar, son. I know how sweet you like it.'

'When did she come?'

His mother shrugged one shoulder ill-humouredly. 'I did not notice the time.'

The servant-boy, a self-satisfied expression on his face, could be seen passing into the bedroom, carrying tea on a tray.

'Why could she not write a letter to say "I am coming",' Prem's mother grumbled.

Prem finished his tea and said, 'I have some writing work to do.'

'Sit here, son,' his mother said. With her own hands she carried the little cane table under the light for him. 'You will not be disturbed here.'

While he was writing she walked round the room on tiptoe. Once she rushed out into the kitchen to admonish the servant-boy who was cheerfully singing: 'My son is doing writing work and you bellow here like a jackal!' When he had finished writing, Prem folded his piece of paper and stuck it into a stamped envelope. He told his mother, 'I must go and post this. It is very important.'

'What is it?'

'It is an application for rise in salary.'

'Go, son,' she said; and sighed, 'How hard my son works.'

Prem walked very quickly to the post-box. The letter he carried was addressed to his sister in Bangalore. It said that Delhi was very hot and their mother's health was suffering; that it would be best for her to be invited to stay in Bangalore; and that they were well and hoped the sister's family was too. He dropped it in the post-box and turned back home. He felt a sense of achievement, and of relief as well.

His mother kept him talking for a long time that evening, so it was late before he could join Indu in the bedroom. She was lying on her side with her back to him, pretending to be asleep. He knew she was only pretending; but it made it difficult to start a conversation with her. He lay down beside her, with his arms clasped behind his head, clearing his throat several times and moving rather ostentatiously to show how very much awake he was. But she gave no sign. At last he said out loud in a cracked voice, 'What did you do all the time when you were away?'

She reacted immediately. She rolled on to her back and said, staring at the ceiling, 'Please don't speak to me.'

'Why?' he said anxiously. 'What is the matter?'

She continued to stare at the ceiling.

'Please tell me what is the matter,' He tried to edge nearer to her but she stuck out her elbow to ward him off, so that he had sadly to sink back again. 'You are angry?' he asked.

'No,' she said furiously.

'You *are* angry,' he said in a tone of discovery.

She kept silent, and he was too bewildered by the fact that she was angry to be able to say anything. After some time, when she had waited long enough for him to question her further, she came out with it herself: 'All evening you sat with your mother.'

'She was talking to me – how could I leave her?'

'Only today I have come back – '

'And I had some writing work to do also.'

'On the day I come back you must sit down to your writing work?'

He kept silent. How could he explain to her? His silence prompted her to further accusation. 'You went out – I heard you.'

'I had to post a letter – it was very important.'

'Yes, now you have important letters to post! But when I am away, not one line could you write to me, though I waited and waited – ' She was sobbing and he comforted her. At first she did not let him, but he would not be pushed off and she did not try very hard. Soon they were both very happy, and felt they belonged together.

Now that she was back, he felt more strongly than ever that the least he could do for her was to earn enough money. She was his wife, and soon she would have his baby, and he had to provide for them both. The thought made him feel proud, though at the same time it brought back all his worries.

He felt he had never yet got really down to the Seigals. He had started off with good intentions several times, but something had always put him off, so that he had never even got as far as hinting at a reduction in rent. Yet it should be so easy – one had merely to divert the stream of neighbourly chat into the required channel. The trouble perhaps was that he did not feel old or mature or settled enough to converse with the Seigals as a neighbourly equal. What was needed was someone older than he, someone whose position commanded more respect, to lay his case before the Seigals. And he at once knew whom he had in mind: his mother. An elderly lady, the widow of a Principal of a college, the mother of a grown-up son and four married daughters – who would not listen to her with attention and respect?

But when he suggested it to her, she said, 'You and your wife go, son', with a weary sigh.

'I want to go with you,' he said. There was some hurry about it too, for she might not be staying much longer.

'Who will listen to a useless old woman like me? Your wife will be able to talk with them much better.'

'Who will listen to her?' Prem said as scornfully as he could, though this did not come easily to him.

His mother kept silent for a while. Then he said, with patience and resignation, 'As you please, son, and began to smooth her hair.

At the Seigals all the lights were blazing and the fans turning and Romesh played film music on the radio. Mr Seigal and three other stout businessmen sat and played cards round a little table. Mrs Seigal crocheted and chatted with other ladies on the veranda. The card players had glasses of whisky beside them; one of them was telling a story: 'So then what happened, this Sardar went to Kakeda Hotel and did the same thing there.' Prem nervously steered his mother out on to the veranda. Her lips were pursed, and she emphatically refused all offers of refreshment.

Mr Seigal held up his whisky glass towards Prem. 'Come and join us!' he shouted.

'My son does not drink spirits,' Prem's mother said at once. The voice in which she spoke this made Prem wish they had not come after all.

The story-teller continued in the expansive leisured tone of one telling a good story: ' "Sardarji", the proprietor of Kakeda Hotel told him, "this is not nice".'

Prem turned hastily to Romesh: 'How are your studies?' But the radio was on too loud for Romesh to hear him.

'How can a boy study and pass in his examinations,' Prem's mother replied instead, 'when there is no peace and quiet in his home?'

'Bring more ice!' Mr Seigal bellowed to the servant in the kitchen.

Mrs Seigal sighed and looked at Romesh: 'His examinations are a great worry to us.' Romesh had a smile of pleasure on his face and he swayed his head in time to the radio music.

'I thank God,' Prem's mother said sternly, 'with my son I never had any worry.'

' "What would happen, Sardarji, if you went to Gaylords and did there what you have done here?" '

'He was always a good boy and studied hard,' Prem's mother said. She stroked Prem's head. He sat quite still, with his hands pushed tight between his knees and his eyes lowered. He thought his mother was working up to the point well: it was good for the Seigals to know how hard-working, well-behaved and altogether deserving he was.

'My Romesh also is a good boy,' said Mrs Seigal, 'but he does not care for his studies.'

'Sardarji replied "It has happened to me already and you know what they said? They said, if this is what you want to do, then don't come to Gaylords, go to Kakeda Hotel!" Ha-ha-ha!' roared the story-teller; he slapped one thigh and looked round expectantly at the others. They also laughed, loudly though rather absentmindedly, for they were busy scanning their cards.

Prem's mother said, 'Of course, my son always had a very peaceful home in which to sit down to his studies.'

'My Romesh likes so much to listen to music on the radio.'

Prem's mother judiciously shook her head. 'In sitting listening to music on the radio, how will he pass in his examinations?'

'It is a great worry,' said Mrs Seigal with a sigh. Prem began to be

110

impatient. They had been here before and they should have progressed a little further to his purpose by this time.

'My son sat down to his studies every day, and sometimes he would sit till late in the night. Of course, his home was very different.' She looked distastefully at the card players, then at the ladies round her enjoying tea and sweetmeats. 'His father was Principal of Ankhpur Government College.'

The card players had now begun an argument which was threatening to become heated. The servant, holding some roughly-hewn ice in a dishcloth, stood and listened to them. 'But you had a spade to put on my queen!' Mr Seigal roared.

'His father used to tell him: "Study, learn and pass in your examinations." That is the sort of home this boy comes from.'

'But at the next turn you played it! A knave of spades it was, I saw!'

Mrs Seigal sighed: 'Why do they play if they only end up in quarrelling?' The servant was peering into each one's cards; the ice was quietly melting through the dishcloth, dripping on to the floor.

'Yes, things were very different for me when my husband was alive,' Prem's mother said. She was already wiping her sari into the corner of her eye. Prem knew that now the subject he had come to discuss would never be reached. 'I was the Principal's wife,' she said. 'Everyone treated me with respect.' Now she was wiping in the corner of her other eye, and Prem realized that it would be some time before he could get her to come home.

Sohan Lal shyly handed Prem an invitation card. 'It is for my younger brother's wedding,' he said. Prem looked at the card which was light green and printed on cheap paper. It was very evidently an invitation to a poor man's wedding.

Sohan Lal watched Prem expectantly, with a shy self-deprecating little smile. Prem laughed nervously; he felt touched and at the same time embarrassed. 'I will certainly come,' he said and looked down again at the shabby little green card. 'It is not too far for you?' Sohan Lal said. The looked away from one another, shy and awkward with each other like a newly married couple. 'I will certainly come,' Prem repeated. He would take Indu. It would be a day's outing for them; they had never had an outing together. He began to look forward to it already. 'My wife and I will both come,' he said, feeling proud. She would wear her platform-sole shoes and jasmine in her hair. He would sit on the bed and watch her dress in front of the mirror. By that time his mother would be gone.

Every day now he expected her to receive a letter from Bangalore. He would come home from the college, eager to see whether she was already packing. But she never was. She sat on the bed and kept him beside her talking for a long time. She never mentioned anything about going away. Indu meanwhile sat alone in the bedroom. Prem wondered what she was thinking in there, but by the time his mother was sleepy and allowed him to go, Indu was usually asleep or pretending to be so; or even if she wasn't, she was quiet and sulky and would hardly talk to him. He became impatient for his sister's letter to arrive.

And in the college he still looked with nervous hopefulness for some result to his petition. But Mr Khanna never gave a sign, though Prem took every opportunity to appear in his way. He was almost forced to the conclusion that Mrs Khanna had failed to hand his letter over. 'Perhaps she forgot,' he told Sohan Lal gloomily; and a bit later, 'Or she did not give it because she was angry with me for interrupting her conversation.' She had, he remembered, looked very angry. Now he did not know what to do, whether to hand over another petition, or try some other method. He was glad he was meeting Raj on Monday. He would be able to consult with Raj: he had begun to regard him as an expert on all matters relating to adult life.

Prem was as usual the first to arrive at their meeting place. He stood in the vestibule of the cinema, among the groups of sleek relaxed young men in bush-shirts and thought of all the things about which he wanted to consult Raj. He was surprised rather than startled when suddenly someone blocked his vision by placing two hands on his eyes from behind. 'Three guesses,' said a voice which he identified at once as Hans's. The hands were very large and damp and smelt of perspiration.

'You are a good guesser,' said Hans. He hooked his arm into Prem's in a friendly manner. 'You are going to the cinema?'

'I am meeting a friend,' Prem mumured.

'Marvellous!' cried Hans and tucked his arm in tighter. 'I will also meet your friend.'

This was something Prem would very much have liked to avoid. He did not think, for one thing, that Hans would make a favourable impression on Raj; and then too, Hans's presence would prevent him from laying his problems before Raj.

'I like to meet the friends of my friends. Friends reveal a person's character and I am a student of the character.' As usual, Hans's voice was loud and uninhibited, and Prem noticed that all the young men standing around were listening with interest. Then I want also to discuss with you what we were talking last time we met. I have been asking myself why it is we cannot control our bad thoughts.' The young men were cocking their ears and nudging one another with their elbows; some of them already wore wide grins. 'Our spirits wish to be pure,' Hans cried, 'but what is it in here that will not let them?' and he drummed his fist on the top of his head in a despairing manner.

'Here is my friend,' Prem said weakly.

Hans clicked the heels of his big black boots together, then joined his hands meekly under his chin. 'Hans Loewe,' he introduced himself to Raj, who stared at him.

'Loewe means lion,' Prem said anxiously.

'I am Prem's good friend,' Hans said. 'I want also to be the friend of his friend.' He grasped Raj by his shoulders and looked down seriously and intently into his face. Raj stared back at him in silent amazement. 'He has a good face,' Hans pronounced at last, turning to Prem, 'but I think he has been neglecting the spiritual side.'

He insisted on taking them to the coffee-house where he had gone with Prem the first time they had met. Prem and Raj followed meekly behind him; they did not look at one another but behaved as if they were only together because they had both been towed along by Hans.

'This is good,' Hans said, settling himself squarely on the settee, his arms planted on the table. 'Today we will have such conversation that our minds will fly open and the understanding will come in with a big rush!' He strained across the table, eager for the conversation to begin.

Prem put his hand on Raj's shoulder and said, 'My friend works in the Ministry of Food. He is a Government officer.' Raj did not say anything. He sat stiffly upright, his arms held close to his body, and stared in front of him.

Hans beamed at him: 'So you are a cog in the vast machinery of the Government?'

'No, I am a sub-officer, Grade Two.'

'By cog I mean one little screw in a big big wheel. It is a joke.' Raj continued to stare ahead of him but now he wore a look of tight-lipped disapproval. Quite obviously he did not regard his job as fit subject for a joke.

113

'He has an important post,' Prem said, mostly to appease Raj, but partly also so as to be able to lead up to talk of his own inadequate job. Perhaps, after all, he would be able to consult Raj about his application for a rise in salary.

Hans said: 'How can a man's work have importance? This is my meaning: work is nothing, only the spirit within is important.' His eyes searched Prem's face, then Raj's. Prem felt constrained to nod and look intelligent. 'If the spirit is pure, all action is pure. How simple it is,' Hans cried, 'how beautiful!' He clasped his hands and looked rapt.

'Your wife has come back from her parents house?' Raj asked.

Prem turned half towards him and nodded. He would like to have turned to him fully, but he also had to show interest in what Hans was saying.

'Please remember that you have invited us for a meal,' Raj said.

'You will come?' Prem exclaimed in a pleased voice.

'Of course, the bus-fares will be an expense for me.'

Hans held up his forefinger again. 'BUT,' he said and smiled: 'Yes, there is always a big BUT.'

'Babli can travel free on the bus,' Prem pointed out.

Raj grudgingly admitted it, then added: 'My wife cannot travel free. I will have to pay for her.'

'But to achieve this pure spirit – yes, there is where we stumble and fall down.' His face had now clouded with unhappiness. 'Our materialist civilization has collected so much waste matter inside us that the spirit has become dirty with mud.'

'You must come very soon,' Prem said. He was about to add, 'as soon as my mother has gone', but then remembered that he was not supposed to know that she was going.

'We are rubbish-dumps!' Hans cried.

Raj said in a stern voice, 'Please don't shout so loud. People will look at us.' Prem cast a hasty glance round the restaurant. But nobody was looking at them. Most of the people there were too intent on themselves to pay attention to what was going on around them.

'What does it matter if people look?' Hans said. 'What we are talking is not a secret thing but the Truth which everyone must know if he is to lead a good spiritual life.'

'They are all loafers,' Raj said with a contemptuous look around the clientele. They were most of them young men, but very different from the young men who lounged, easy and satisfied, in the vestibules of the cinemas. These young men sat over their coffee with an air of cynical gloom, and the way they blew cigarette smoke indicated their low opinion of the world.

'Perhaps they are already on the path of the Truth,' Hans said.

'They are all worthless loafers,' Raj said. 'They sit in coffee-houses and do no work the whole day.'

Prem said, 'Perhaps they can't find work. It is not easy to find work, even if you are B.A. or M.A.'; and he gently sighed, thinking of the long columns of Situations Vacant in which there was nothing for him.

Raj frowned at his watch: 'I must go. I have to get clothes from the dry-cleaner on my way home.'

'And even if you do get work,' Prem said, 'often the salary is so low that it difficult to live.'

'I have a theory,' Hans announced.

'Especially if you have a family to support,' Prem mumured.

'My theory is that where there is greatest unemployment among the educated classes there is also greatest spiritual development.'

'And it is so difficult to get a rise in salary,' Prem said miserably.

'Yes, I know, my theory sounds very strange,' Hans said with a pleased laugh. 'But I will explain.'

Raj got up. 'If I don't hurry, the dry-cleaner will shut and we will be without our clothes.'

Prem got up with him and said, 'There were some things I wanted to talk with you about.'

'I was very happy to have this meeting with you,' Hans said. He clasped Raj's hand in a big firm handshake. Now all three of them were standing and the waiter came hurring over with the bill.

'I sent a petition to the Principal,' Prem told Raj. But Hans put a hand on his shoulder and pressed him back into his seat. 'Now I will explain my theory,' he said; he was smiling and his eyes too gleamed with pleasure.

Prem's mother was sitting on her bed, looking at the letter in her hand. She said, 'Here is a letter for me from your sister in Bangalore.'

'What does she say?' Prem asked casually, fingering the morning paper which lay folded on a chair.

'Please don't be angry with me, son.'

Prem pretended to be interested in the newspaper although he had already read it very thoroughly in the morning.

'Your sister needs me, son. I will have to leave you.' She opened the letter again and glanced over it and nodded. 'What can I do, son? She needs me.'

Prem looked crestfallen, but he said bravely, 'Of course if she needs you, you must go.'

'A mother's duties never end,' she said with a sigh. But she looked pleased.

So next evening Prem saw her off at the station. She had as many baskets and bundles as she had brought with her when she came, for she was taking a good supply of Delhi sweetmeats to her daughter. When she was settled in her compartment and had seen to it that the porter had stowed all her things properly on the racks, she spoke to Prem out of the window. She said, 'I am not easy in my mind about leaving you, son.'

'Please don't worry at all,' Prem said. He stepped nearer to the train, for barrows filled with mail-bags were being pushed along the platform.

'I did my best for you, son. We chose the girl as carefully as we could.'

Prem said again, 'Please don't worry about me at all.' He was embarrassed, afraid that she would say something about Indu and then he would not know where to look.

'However careful we are, what can we do? These things are all in the hands of God.' A group of women, fat and elderly and wearing widow-white, came thronging into the compartment. They were followed by a porter who carried their luggage on his head and looked despondently at the racks into which Prem's mother had crowded all her things. 'Someone has taken up all the space,' said one of the women.

'For one seat one must take up only one luggage rack,' said another.

'Try and bear up, son,' Prem's mother told him.

He cleared his throat and said, 'I think some of your things must be moved.'

The porter was already gingerly moving them. Prem's mother pretended not to notice what was going on.

'If I could stay with you, son, I would look after you and make everything nice for you. Then there would be no need for worry.'

'*Film-Fun, Film-Fare, Film-Frolic!*' shouted a paperman, thrusting

116

a splayed-out array of highly coloured film magazines into the train window.

'But what to do? Your sister needs me.' She drew back from the magazines thrust into her face, saying 'Go away, what do I want with these things.'

'It is all about films,' said the man invitingly.

One of the fat widows shook her head: 'That is all young people think of nowadays. Only films.' The others also shook their heads. One of them was already untying a little bundle on her lap out of which came a heap of potato pancakes. She began to eat at once. With a full mouth she said, 'It is a great evil.'

Prem's mother said, 'I thank God, my son is not like that. He is a good hard-working boy.' The other women stared at Prem in appreciation and said 'Ah', swaying their heads at him and smiling.

'He has been married less than a year. I have been staying with him.' She sighed. 'What help a mother can give, I have given.'

'What can compare with a mother's love?' the others said politely.

Prem looked towards the end of the train: 'I think it is starting.'

One of the fat women came pushing to the window. 'It is starting? We have not had our tea!' She began gesticulating to a man with a glass-trolley from which he served tea and biscuits and dust-flecked cream-rolls. Soon steaming cups and heaped plates passed between the trolley and the compartment.

'Now his sister from Bangalore has written to say she needs me. That is why I have to go.' The women were busy eating and drinking, but they nodded sympathetically. 'It is difficult for me to leave this boy, but what can I do?'

The man with the glass trolley was looking nervously at the women drinking tea from his cups and eating off his plates. 'It is starting,' he said. Prem peered towards the engine. His mother said, I run from one to the other, all our lives our children need us'; she tried to sound harassed but her tone was complacent.

'Please give me my things!' shouted the man with the trolley from behind Prem. Flags were being waved and whistles blown.

'He wants his cups and plates,' Prem said.

'I tried to teach her your favourite dishes, son,' Prem's mother said. 'But she does not learn well.'

'Your biscuits are very bad!' one of the women shouted to the man with the trolley.

'But give me my things!' he shouted back.

'He wants his things,' Prem said.

'I have done all I could, son. The rest is in God's hands.'

Cups and plates were passed out to Prem, who handed them on to the man with the trolley. The train started. Prem ran alongside it, with the trolleyman behind him.

'If your sister had not needed me, I would have stayed with you a much longer time.'

Prem received the last two cups.

'There was not enough sugar in your tea!' one of the women cried, leaning out of the window.

Prem's mother also leant out of the window: 'Try and bear up, son!' she cried.

Prem waved and said, 'Please don't worry at all', though it was not likely that she could any longer hear.

He did not wait till the train was out of sight but turned straightaway and made his way to the exit. He was so excited that he hardly noticed the crowds milling round the station-yard and kept stumbling against porters and hawkers and passengers, over mail-bags and abandoned clusters of luggage, and once he almost slipped on a sucked and discarded mango-peel. He thought only of getting home as quickly as possible, where Indu would be sitting waiting for him.

In the night they went to sleep out on the roof. They felt both alone and supreme. The sky, vaulting huge and black above them, nailed with silver points of stars and a slice of moon, seemed closer than the earth. Sounds of cars, the bark of a dog, a distant train reached them faint and filtered and far-off. He tried to persuade her to take off all her clothes and show herself naked to him. She blushed, giggled, clutched the sari defensively to her breast, while he tried to pull it off. They struggled together and then they loved one another. Never had they known such an excess of sweetness. Cloyed and sated, they slept together on the bed. Later they woke up again and loved some more. After that they did not go to sleep for a long time; the night was large and silent and empty, and they did not want to lose a moment of the feeling of space and solitude it gave them. They peered over the roof down into the courtyard where Mr Seigal lay sleeping alone on a string-cot, with an earthen water-container by his side. They could see his stomach curving like a dome into the air. Silvered in faint moonlight, he did not look like a real person at all. They went to sleep towards early morning, when the sky was already grey with dawn, but soon afterwards the servant-boy stood there, saying crossly, 'I have been searching for you everywhere.' They woke up and noticed that the hot sun was shining on them, so they went running indoors.

Even in the daytime, at college, Prem thought mostly of Indu and what they did together. He gave his lessons automatically, while his thoughts were on her. His students did not bother to listen to him. They held their own conversations, leaning across to one another and hardly bothering to lower their voices. Prem remained unaware of this, until suddenly Mr Chaddha interrupted the flow of his own lecture on 'Conflicts in the North-West Frontier Provinces' to say in his sharp piping voice: 'There is too much noise on the other side of the classroom.'

There was instant silence. Mr Chaddha's students turned round to have a look at Prem's, who now sat quite quiet and pretended to be engrossed in their notes.

From his dais at one end of the class-room Prem faced Mr Chaddha on his dais at the other. Prem said, 'I was giving my lecture', in a shaking voice.

'Perhaps you were giving your lecture but your students don't seem to have been listening to you,' Mr Chaddha said.

Prem felt rebuked like a schoolboy. He hung his head and plucked at the notes in front of him. There was a heavy silence, during which Prem felt his disgrace mounting. At last Mr Chaddha resumed his lecture and his students turned back. Prem also continued to speak, though he could not remember where he had left off before Mr Chaddha's interruption. His students remained more quiet than he had ever known them for the rest of the lesson; nevertheless Prem was greatly relieved when it was over.

But a sense of shame remained with him. He had been publicly disgraced and made to lose face before his students. He felt it acutely. He knew he was not very successful at keeping discipline – indeed not very successful at teaching – but this was a fact that should be kept decently hidden. No man could hope for standing and respect if his weaknesses were exposed. His sense of shame began to be mingled with some indignation. He realized that Mr Chaddha had really no right to administer any rebuke to him, let alone disgrace him as he had done in front of all their students. Prem was himself a teacher, a husband, a householder, and as such some respect was due to him.

His indignation increased when he saw Mr Chaddha sitting in his usual position in an armchair in the middle of the staffroom, with his little legs crossed and one foot swinging free in the air. He was reading a book with his usual air of pompous authoritativeness. Without thinking at all, Prem went straight up to him and said in a voice trembling with resentment, 'It is not nice to disgrace a teacher in front of his students.'

Mr Chaddha lowered his book and glanced up at Prem standing accusingly in front of him. Prem noticed that he wore a look of astonishment.

'If you wish to tell me something, you can tell me quietly after the lesson!' Prem cried, close to tears.

Mr Chaddha's look of astonishment gave way to one of extreme annoyance. He said, 'You will please lower your voice when you speak to me.'

Prem cried, 'I can speak to you any way I like! I am not your student, I am a teacher!' His voice was shrill. He put up his hand and, ashamed and impatient, brushed a tear from his cheekbone.

Mr Chaddha rose from his armchair. He rose with the slow and terrible dignity of a figure of vengeance, though his short stature made it end in rather an anti-climax. 'Unheard-of!' he brought out in fearful wrath.

The other teachers were listening breathlessly, though they were half turned away from the scene and watching only from the corner of their eyes. No one wished to be involved.

'What is impertinence?' Prem cried shrilly. 'To make a teacher look small before his students – perhaps that is not impertinence?'

'Gross impudence!' cried Mr Chaddha.

'Don't speak to me like that!' Prem shrilled, balling his fists and stamping one foot.

'Unprecedented insolence!' cried Mr Chaddha. Puffing and snorting, he began to pace up and down the staff-room with quick angry little steps. 'This is a matter for the Principal.'

'It is not right for a teacher – '

'I shall make a full report to the Principal,' said Mr Chaddha, pacing and puffing.

'Then make report, what do I care!' Prem cried in tearful defiance. But it was not a defiance he could quite feel: the idea of Mr Chaddha reporting to the Principal was not pleasant to him. Especially just now when he hoped Mr Khanna was considering his petition and nothing must be allowed to prejudice him in that delicate task.

'I shall point out to him how my own lectures are disturbed because of indiscipline at the other end of the class-room.'

'What indiscipline? How can you say indiscipline?' Prem said; his voice had become milder, even anxious.

But Mr Chaddha was not to be deflected. 'A full report shall be made,' he said, intent on his own indignation. Only the bell stopped him pacing up and down the room. He gathered up his notes at once; in the doorway he stopped still and announced in a fateful voice, 'The end of this has not yet been heard.'

The other teachers hurried away. No one said anything. Prem walked along the corridor with Sohan Lal who also did not say anything. Though he would have appreciated some words of sympathy and support, Prem understood that Sohan Lal could not afford to get involved by taking sides.

All the way home he felt uneasy. Not so much because of the disgrace in the classroom; or because of the unpleasantness of his scene with Mr Chaddha; but because of the possible consequence of these things. If Mr Chaddha really reported to the Principal and drew his attention to the fact that Prem was not very good at maintaining discipline, then Mr Khanna might not be as favourably disposed towards an increase in salary as Prem now hoped he was.

He worried till he got home: but then he forgot all about it, for Indu was singing in the kitchen. When she saw him, she pretended to be annoyed. 'You are so early – I have not finished any of my work yet,' she said, trying to sound busy and flustered. But he saw that she had already had her evening bath and was wearing a fresh sari and her scent like vanilla essence, and her hair was newly brushed and oiled. He tried to embrace her. 'Go away,' she said; 'have you no shame, in the middle of the day?' 'What does it matter?' he murmured into her scented neck. 'Who can see us?' She smelt so fresh, with soap and scent, and yet underneath that there was her own deep woman-smell. 'Let me go,' she said, half-heartedly pushing against his chest. The servant-boy was vigorously sweeping the stairs – swish, went his broom, and in time with it he chanted a counting-out rhyme.

So it was not until next morning, on his way back to the college, that Prem remembered to worry again. By that time he thought it unlikely that Mr Chaddha had done anything so drastic as reporting to Mr Khanna, so his thoughts centred mainly on whether his request for an increase in salary would be granted or not. Though he was by no means sure that Mrs Khanna had handed the petition on. He would give Mr Khanna three more days; if he had heard nothing from him after that, then he would really have to write another petition.

But he did not have to wait that long. For with the tea that morning, the servant brought a note which asked Prem to come up and see the Principal. Prem became quite excited; he showed the note to Sohan Lal, saying: 'It must be about my increase in salary.' He smoothed his collar, ran a comb through his hair, patted his cheek to see if he had a nice close shave. He wanted to look his best.

'Ah, yes,' said Mr Khanna. Mrs Khanna was sitting at the table with her knees wide apart; she was painting her finger-nails.

Prem felt very nervous. So much depended on Mr Khanna's decision. He was smiling half expectantly, half fearfully, but he was unaware of this.

'Well, yes now,' said Mr Khanna.

Prem croaked, 'You sent for me,' still smiling.

Mrs Khanna said, 'What time is the train arriving?'

'Let me talk,' Mr Khanna said irritably. To Prem he said, 'Quite right, I sent for you.'

'Thank you, sir,' Prem said.

'There has been a complaint against you,' Mr Khanna said.

The smile came off Prem's face. This was not what he thought he had come for. He felt betrayed.

'It seems you don't keep discipline in your class and consequently other classes are disturbed.'

'I am only asking so I know what time we have to go to the station,' Mrs Khanna said.

'This college has always been noted for its excellent discipline,' Mr Khanna said with a severe sincerity, as if he were challenging someone to contradict him.

'Will it be after our tea or before?' Mrs Khanna asked.

'Why don't you let me do my work!' Mr Khanna turned on her. She continued to paint her nails with pursed lips and an air of dignity.

'We have always had a most distinguished and reliable teaching staff,' Mr Khanna said, and again he made it sound as if it were true.

'I cannot allow,' he went on, 'any weak link in the college.' He struck the table with his knuckles so that Mrs Khanna's bottles of nail polish shook: 'You are a weak link,' he accused.

Prem wanted to say something, to justify himself and show Mr

Khanna that it was a mistake and he was not a weak link at all. But he was too deeply shocked to be able to speak.

'If you wish to stay with us,' Mr Khanna said, 'you will have to improve yourself.' Mrs Khanna nodded in agreement. 'Certainly he has a lot to improve,' she said, without looking up from her nails.

'I cannot undertake to pay out a monthly salary to someone who is not worthy of his hire,' Mr Khanna said.

'Everyone must be worthy of his hire,' said Mrs Khanna.

'I have the reputation of this college to consider,' said Mr Khanna. 'The parents of my pupils expect me to provide a first-class teaching staff.'

Mrs Khanna said, 'Today I must have the staffroom cleared out for our guests.'

'I can only keep up our high standard if every member of my staff pulls his weight.'

'I will bring down the guest towels and sheets in the afternoon after our food. Before that it must be properly cleaned out and aired.'

'Why do you keep interrupting me?' Mr Khanna shouted.

'Who is interrupting?' she shouted back.

'Please remember what I have said,' Mr Khanna told Prem. 'I cannot give a second warning. That will be all,' he said sternly but Prem still stood there, dazed.

'What do you mean – interrupting you? Perhaps now I should neglect all my household matters!'

'You can go now!' Mr Khanna told Prem in a loud voice.

The fear of losing his job was a new one for Prem. He knew he was not very good at teaching, but he had never thought that this short-coming might lead to his dismissal. It was not as if he shirked his duties – he was always there on time, never missed a lesson, hardly ever left before five. What more could he do? It was not his fault that he had not been born a good teacher. People should make allowances for one another's weaknesses.

When he realized that Mr Khanna was not disposed to make allowances and that he might even dismiss him, he was very much afraid. His mind leapt to the consequences of dismissal: the difficulty – or even impossibility – of finding another job, the destitution of himself, Indu and their baby. They would have to give up their own flat and go and live with one after another of their relations. Perhaps they would have more children, and everyone would be angry with him and say:

'He earns not a pai to keep himself and still he loads his wife with children.' Indu would have to sell all her pieces of jewellery, her satin blouses and fine saris would become old and frayed and she would have no money to buy new ones.

He knew that, whatever it might cost him, he had to hold on to his job. He had to do everything, accept everything, for the sake of holding on to his job. He had to be like Sohan Lal, quiet, patient, self-effacing, in the effort not to come under displeasurable notice; constantly alert not to offend.

He felt the weight of this new burden so heavily that not even Indu could lighten it. His pensive and melancholy mood made her think that he was annoyed with her and she withdrew from him and sulked by herself.

They were both sitting on the bed, both with their backs supported against the headrest with the entwined cupids, both with their legs drawn up and their eyes staring at the patchily whitewashed wall of their tiny bedroom. At last, with a sigh, he held out his hand towards her: 'Come here,' he said softly.

She did not move, only folded her arms to show obstinate defiance.

'Please come to me,' he said.

'Why should I come to you? When you don't want me, you sit quiet by yourself and I am nothing, some wooden toy perhaps, nothing more, but when you want me, I must run.'

'Who said I did not want you?'

'Then why do you sit by yourself like that – no, don't come near to me! I don't like you!' But he came all the same. He said: 'I was thinking. You don't understand – '

'I see. Thank you. I don't understand. I am stupid.'

'What can I say to you?' he said, half laughing, while he tried to kiss her.

'Let me tell you, I am not stupid at all! On the contrary, when I was in the school, all the teachers said Indu can study very well if she tries, she has a good brain!'

'Yes, yes, I know.' He was full of tenderness for her. The fact that he knew about the insecurity that would for ever threaten them and she did not, made him feel very loving towards her. He wanted to keep her innocent and unsuspecting, and to protect her.

'In sums I was not so very good, but in reading and writing I was always first in the class! Oh, you there!' she called to the servant-boy.

'Why do you call him now?' Prem said and tried to kiss her again.

'If I don't think of your food, then who will? Just see the lentils don't boil over,' she instructed the servant-boy.

'Were you quarrelling with him?' the boy asked.

'I have never seen such an impertinent – Get out!' she shouted, which he did in a hurry. She grumbled, 'I would like to tear the skin from him with my nails', while Prem kissed her quite passionately.

But when he was away from her, all his melancholy thoughts came back. He even began to think rather longingly of his boyhood again: of living in his father's house, looked after by his mother and with no responsibilities except those of passing in his examinations. Yet he knew he did not want that at all. He wanted to be looked after not by his mother but by Indu. And he wanted to look after her.

But he was weak and alone. He was on one side with Indu behind him and the coming baby, and on the other side were the Khannas and the Seigals and Mr Chaddha and his students and doctor's bills and income tax forms and all the other horrors the world had in store for him. He felt that he was required to pit his strength against all these, and yet he knew from the beginning that it was hopeless because he did not have much strength. He knew that the only way he could survive was by submitting to and propitiating the other side.

These gloomy thoughts accompanied him to the college and back home again. On his return he found Mr Seigal standing on the porch, looking out at the weather and probing at a tooth. 'The monsoon should not be long now,' he told Prem.

Prem stood beside him and also looked out at the weather. He felt small and weak beside Mr Seigal, who was tall with a big head and a big stomach thrust far in front of him.

'Another week perhaps,' said Mr Seigal, concentrating on a cavity in his mouth and trying to pull something out of it.

'Yes, I think so,' said Prem. He was trembling with nervousness, but all the same he said, 'I find your rent very high for me,' Mr Seigal.'

Mr Seigal thrust his head back in an effort to get deeper into the tooth.

'My salary is not very big and it is difficult for me to pay so much rent every month.'

'Ai,' said Mr Seigal in irritation at his tooth and digging deeper.

'Especially now I expect my expenses to go up higher.' Prem looked out into the street where a man was passing with a barrowful of little cut cubes of sugar-cane. 'Perhaps you know already – you see, I am

125

expecting,' he cleared his throat, 'my wife is expecting a baby,' he said and scuffed his feet. Mr Seigal said 'Ah' as he dislodged the offending particle; then he said 'Very nice', and slapped Prem on the back; 'let us hope for a boy.'

'Thank you,' Prem said.

'Though nowadays, what does it matter – boy, girl, it is all the same. Very nice,' he said again and went indoors.

Prem had not really expected anything better. He realized that no one was interested in his difficulties, that the problem of supporting himself and Indu and any family they might have was his alone. The harshness of the world filled him with bitterness and despondency. It seemed to him that adult, settled, worldly people – people like Mr Khanna and Mr Seigal – should be glad and even eager to help a young man just starting out in life and with a family to support. But nobody cared. 'Wherever you look in the world,' he told Sohan Lal, 'people think only of themselves and they don't love their neighbours at all.' Sohan Lal looked sad in sympathy. 'Everywhere there is selfishness and even cruelty, so that it is very difficult for a young man to make his way.' Sohan Lal nodded and sighed; then he said, 'I am going to see Swamiji this evening; you will come?' Prem at once said he would. He wondered he had not thought of it himself. With the swami there would be an escape, for however brief a time, from his sense of the world's oppression.

The swami had many visitors. People sat tightly packed against one another on the floor, and some stood against the walls and some were even out on the staircase. Prem and Sohan Lal managed to get in and to find room to sit on the floor. The swami waved and smiled to them and seemed very pleased they had come, though he did not say anything to them. The room was perfumed with incense and there were fruits and orange flower-garlands and a basketful of rose petals.

The fat Sethji, whom Prem had seen on his first visit, sat near the swami. He wore immaculate clothes of fine white muslin. There was a melancholy expression on his face, and he was saying: 'I often think, if I could start again from the beginning, I too would give my whole life for the love of God.'

Vishvanathan, the tall, dark, angry young man, said, 'And what is stopping you now?'

Sethji shrugged. 'What can I tell you?' he said.

'I know what you will tell me,' Vishvanathan said. 'You will tell me that you have a wife and children and many commitments, daughters

126

to marry and younger brothers to educate and widowed sisters to support. You will also tell me that there are many charities and other good works which depend on you, and for the sake of these you cannot leave off all your activities. Isn't that so?'

Sethji said, 'I have come to listen to Swamiji, not to you.'

'Well, answer me at least,' Vishvanathan said with a laugh.

'Answer him,' the swami smilingly urged. 'Sometimes he also knows a little sense.'

Sethji told Vishvanathan, 'What can I say to you? What do you understand of responsibilities which eat up a man's life so that it is no longer his own life?'

'Only this,' said Vishvanathan. 'That they are no stronger than threads of cotton compared with the responsibilities you have to God.'

'It is easy enough for you to talk,' Sethji said.

'And I will tell you something more!' Vishvanathan cried, loud enough to drown other voices which had begun to contribute to the conversation. 'If once you feel your responsibility to God – which is nothing more than the responsibility to love Him – if you feel it once, only once, strong enough, here and here and here' – and he sharply struck his head and his chest and his belly with the flat of his hand – 'then at once you will forget everything you now think so important, and you will let it go and never even think of looking back!'

He spoke with such fire and truth that there was no place for argument. In the silence that followed, his words echoed in many minds. Prem felt himself much moved. He imagined how it would strike him, this love for God, and how he would leave everything and everyone behind him and devote himself to that alone. So sweet was this vision, so tempting and rapturous, that he had no regrets for what he would leave behind him; not even for Indu.

The swami said, 'When I was a boy, I was like all the other mischievous boys in the village. I stole mangoes from the trees, I licked curds from the bowl, I cut down the fish hung up to dry. In the village they named me the Wild One. Then God called me.' He was smiling, and yet there were tears in his eyes. 'I left my village and I spent my time thinking of Him. I wanted Him to possess me entirely and to make me one with Him. But sometimes it was hard. I could not get a vision of Him and this tormented me. I would throw myself on the ground and beat it with my fists and drum my feet like a naughty child. I cursed Him and scolded Him and told Him I would kill myself because He did not want me. But then, at these moments, when I was sunk so deep in anguish that I thought I would never be able to rise from it again, then God would call me. Gently, softly, like the mother calls her child. He called me; and at once I was comforted and I was good again, as the child is good when it is restored to the embrace and forgiveness of the mother.'

Sethji said sadly, 'He does not call everyone.'

'He has called you,' Vishvanathan said. 'Only you don't want to hear.'

'No,' the swami said, 'he wants to hear but the world is too loud in his ears.'

Prem felt a desire to cry, I also want to hear! He thought he could if he wanted to, and at that moment it seemed to him that it would be easy to still the noise of the world in his ears. He was sitting quiet on the floor, with his legs tucked under him and his hands folded, but inwardly he trembled with new longings.

Someone began to sing. He sang: 'You have many good sons on earth, O Mother, few fickle as I; and yet, O gracious one, it is not right for you to abandon me; a son may be bad, but never a mother.' Everyone sat silent and listened. The voice was low and unemphatic but sonorous with feeling; it inspired at the same time both peace and longing. Prem looked at the swami, who sat crosslegged on the bed, his eyes half shut in ecstasy, his mouth open with the tip of the tongue protruding; and from him he looked at Vishvanathan, sitting on the ground at the foot of the bed, with his head erect and an expression of calm and certainty on his face. And Prem felt that his own life too had, like a river, found its own bed and was running with theirs in one current towards God.

But next morning he was thinking mainly of his job and his rent. Indu said, 'You always look cross', watching him step into his trousers.

'I have many worries,' he sighed.

'What worries? It is I who have many worries.'

'You also have worries?'

'Of course,' she said, rather proudly. He smiled and quickly bit her neck. 'Get away from me!' she cried.

He finished dressing and combed his hair in front of the mirror. He studied his face and noted, not without satisfaction, that it was a man's face, no longer a boy's. 'Shall I grow a moustache?' he said.

Indu covered her face and rocked with laughter.

'What is funny? I think I shall look quite nice.'

Indu threw herself on the bed. 'Oh,' she gasped, 'now he wants to become a film star!' She rolled herself from side to side. Prem watched her for a while, smiling, then he could bear it no longer and fell on top of her, covering her face and neck with kisses. 'You are tickling me!' she panted; but soon she stopped laughing and they were both very passionate.

Afterwards, as always when they had loved one another in the daytime, they were rather shamefaced. She helped him straighten the collar of his shirt and, with her face averted from him, murmured, 'You will be late for your college.' She accompanied him to the top of the stairs; suddenly, just as he was about to go down, she said, 'I have been thinking something.'

'What have you been thinking?'

'I have been thinking . . .' She stood and twisted her hands.

'Please hurry, I have to go to the college.'

'We have never had any guests.'

Prem laughed. 'I will invite guests for you.'

'Really?' she said. 'When?'

He was already half-way down the stairs. 'Soon!' he called, without looking back at her.

She leant over the banister. 'What shall I cook for them?' And though she could no longer see him: 'Will they like pilao, do you think?'

At lunchtime, on his way back from the college, Prem stepped in at the Seigals to use the telephone. He met no one except Romesh, who lay fast asleep on the floor with the fan blowing on him full blast. Mrs Seigal could be heard having an argument with her servant in the kitchen. At the other end of the line Raj sounded cross: 'You should not telephone to me in the office. It will create a bad impression.'

Prem said formally: 'I am telephoning to invite you and your family to eat with us at one o-clock on Sunday, the twenty-second.'

'The bus fare will come very expensive for me.'

'I hope you will honour me by accepting this invitation,' Prem said.

There was a short pause at the other end; then Raj said, 'Oh all right,' and added grudgingly, 'Thank you.'

Prem replaced the receiver, feeling proud and pleased. Now, when he and Indu had cooked for and entertained their own guests, they would have grown to their full stature of householders and married couple.

*

The evening before they were to go to Sohan Lal's brother's wedding, the rains broke. Prem and Indu flung open all their windows and then they ran up on the roof to bathe in the rain. Water trickled from their hair and down their faces and soaked into their clothes. They laughed and ran round and round the roof and flapped their arms. Afterwards they rubbed themselves with towels, laughing and panting, their eyes and noses glistening, their hair clinging in wet coils. Water came dripping through the ceiling in the bedroom and they had to set a saucepan underneath to catch it. Prem looked up at the defective ceiling and shook his head: 'Forty-five rupees rent a month, and the water comes in.'

Indu was wiping her hair with a towel. Suddenly she said, 'If it rains like this tomorrow, how can I wear my georgette sari and my platform-sole shoes to the wedding?' She appeared rather worried for the rest of the evening.

But though it rained all night, by next morning it had stopped. Indu took a long time to get dressed. She stood in front of the mirror and was very critical of herself. Prem, ready long before her, sprawled across the bed, his head supported on his hand, and watched her with a great deal of pleasure. She wore a fine flimsy lilac-coloured sari, spangled all over with silver stars, and a lilac-coloured blouse of satin that shone like a mirror; though she had draped her sari as loosely as possible, it did nothing to hide the swelling splendour of her pregnant belly and breasts.

It was a long bus-ride to Mehrauli. Since it was Sunday, the bus was almost empty; there were only a few solitary old men and one solitary old woman clutching a dirty little cloth bundle on her lap. The conductor sat on the front seat writing a letter though the bus, which was old and loose, rattled a good deal. Prem and Indu sat side by side; Indu looked out of the window and Prem looked mostly straight ahead of him. They did not talk all the way, for they would have felt it to be indelicate to have a conversation together in public. They were also careful to sit far enough apart never to come into contact with one another, however much the bus rattled and shook them.

They found the countryside wet and juicy-green with the night's rain. The air looked liquid and the birds too sang like water. The sky was massing dark blue – soon there would be more rain. But now it was very still; raindrops trembled like dew on the freshened leaves.

'Do you know the way?' Indu said.

'He told me go past the lake –

'There is the lake.' It was swollen with water. A group of women in bright reds and yellows squatted on the bank, washing clothes. They pounded the clothes on stones with vigorous arms raised high, and at the same time they chatted and laughed in shrill voices. On the far bank, hovering on the edge of the lake like a lotus, was a crumbling little stone pavilion.

'I hope it is not far,' Indu said. 'There is something in my shoe.'

'You can take it out,' Prem said. Off the road, set among shrubs and bushes, were some old grey mausoleums. He led her to one of them and she sat down on the steps and took off her shoe. 'It was a stone,' she said.

He stood above her, supporting himself against a pillar. 'It is nice here,' he said. He looked with pleasure at the lush grass, the bushes heavy with rain, the swollen lake. 'And rents are cheap,' he said. But he knew that he did not want to come and live here. It was pleasant for a day's outing, but he was too proud of having established himself in a big town like Delhi, with buses and tongas and coffee-houses and many cinemas, ever to want to change it for a place like Mehrauli. To have done so would have been a step backwards for him; almost like going back to Ankhpur.

Indu looked up at the sky. 'If it rains, my clothes will be spoilt,' she said anxiously. She put back her shoes and they walked on. A group of children came scampering up, shouting, 'They are going to the wedding!' They skipped beside and in front of them, escorting them into the village street. It was a narrow winding street with open booths on both sides – booths selling embroidered slippers, booths selling cheap cotton cloth, booths selling vegetables or fruits or sweetmeats or chunks of meat hung up on hooks. Over the shops were wooden verandas and arched windows set in thin crumbling walls. Prem and Indu, escorted by the troupe of triumphant children, walked down the street with the measured dignity of invited wedding guests.

'Up here!' cried the children. They stood aside, grinning, while Prem and Indu walked into a dark doorway by the side of a booth selling coloured drinks in bottles. The stairs too were very dark. Upstairs Sohan Lal met them; he was excited and rather flustered but glad to see them. Indu was taken off to join the women, and Prem, catching a glimpse into the room where the women sat, noticed how she was received with the deference due to a pregnant woman, with appraising looks and a special solicitude for her comfort. This made him feel rather proud.

The men were congregated in a long bare room overlooking the street. No one talked much, and there was an air of constraint about the whole party; evidently the hosts were not used to entertaining nor the guests to being entertained. The bridegroom sat silent and unregarded on a chair. He wore a long white silken coat and a pink turban from which streams of orange flowers dangled over his face. He was cracking his finger joints. Near him sat a group of old men with hollow grey-stubbled cheeks and scraggy leathery necks rising out of their best shirts; they were discussing the price of grain in desultory tones.

Downstairs in the street the band struck up. 'Ah,' said the old men, raising their heads to listen. 'It is time to go,' they said. Sohan Lal peered out of the window at the band below. He rubbed his hands, smiled and said in an uncertain voice, 'Yes, time to go.' The guests got up but as there was no one to lead the way, they only stood around and looked embarrassed. The bridegroom remained on his chair and stared down at his own shoes. Then a woman's voice called from outside the door, 'Come! What are you doing?' and everyone at once began moving. Sohan Lal motioned to the bridegroom, who got up and let himself be led downstairs. The horse on which he was to ride to the house of the bride was already waiting outside the cold-drink stall. He was helped on to it, watched all along the street by delighted children, by bored shopkeepers sitting inside their booths and women peeping out from upstairs windows.

Prem stood inside the doorway with the other wedding guests and remembered, with great poignancy, his own wedding. He thought he knew just how the bridegroom was feeling. He had caught a glimpse of his face through the streams of flowers dangling down from the turban and had noted the expression of numb endurance. That was how he too had felt, on the day they had married him to Indu. He had not, when it had come to that ultimate point, wanted to be married at all. So he had let everything happen around him – the sweetmeats, the flowers, the band, the coloured lights, the excited bejewelled women – and had sat silent and withdrawn. He had, he remembered, felt rather resentful. Why should he be taken to be married to this girl whom he had seen only once and whom he had not found at all pretty? And he had been afraid too. He had known that, from that day on, everything would be different for him.

The band, which consisted of only four men in frayed uniforms, struck up again. The bridegroom sat lowering upon his horse. Then it began to rain. A few fat raindrops came splashing down, threatening more to come. 'Hurry now, hurry!' everyone shouted. The women, shimmering in silks and satins, came out of the house and bundled into the horse-carriages which had been ordered for them, though the bride's house was only a short way up the street. Prem caught a brief look at Indu and saw how the other women solicitiously helped her up into the carriage. The band played merrily and the bridegroom sat stoic and unmoving while the rain came down and soaked into his fine clothes and garlands. The procession moved forward rather hurriedly. Children skipped alongside and two very dirty pariah dogs stood and barked at the band. Prem's heart leapt with the gay wedding music, and he looked at the glum bridegroom and smiled with superior knowledge.

Prem's behaviour at the college was nowadays very circumspect. He avoided contact with Mr and Mrs Khanna as much as he had formerly sought it. Far from wishing to be noticed for his good qualities, he now wanted only, like Sohan Lal, not to be noticed at all. He taught his classes as well as he could and though this was not, he knew, very well, yet he was satisfied as long as his students did not make their inattentiveness too noticeable. He had ceased actively to hope for a rise in salary; all he wanted was not to lose his job.

He was not pleased when, one day, in the middle of his lecture, the door of the classroom opened and Hans came walking in. True, Hans tried to create as little disturbance as possible by walking with big silent strides on the tips of his boots, hunching his head between his shoulders and laying an admonitory forefinger on his lips. But he was not, even with these mollifying precautions, a figure easily ignored. He was wearing shorts laced at the sides with green string and held up with embroidered braces; on his feet he had large nailed boots which creaked as he tried silently to progress. He slid into an empty seat and sat there, all attentiveness, his hands folded on the desk, his head laid in a listening attitude to one side. Prem's students craned to stare at him, they nudged one another, tittered and discussed him in urgent whispers. Prem cleared his throat and then raised his voice: 'The inseparable preposition *sa* is more often used in poetry than in colloquial Hindi.' Only Hans seemed to be listening. He nodded and looked intelligent, intent only on the lecturer and apparently oblivious of the students who were taking such an interest in him all around.

When at last the bell rang for the end of the lesson, Hans rose, beaming, and advanced towards Prem. 'I wanted to hear you lecture,' he said. 'That is why I have come creeping in quiet like a mouse.' Prem threw an uneasy glance at his students, who stood expectantly smiling. 'My lessons are finished now,' Prem said, making for the door.

Hans followed him. 'What a nice college,' he said. 'It is so home-like. Let me go and see upstairs.' The students had now followed them into the corridor and other students, coming out of other classroom, also stopped to look.

'The Principal lives upstairs,' Prem said.

'Good, I would like to meet.'

'Move along there now,' cried Mr Chaddha testily, emerging from the classroom and finding the corridor blocked with students who had stopped to look at them.

'This is your colleague?' Hans asked with genuine pleasure. He advanced on Mr Chaddha with outstretched hand: 'I am Hans Loewe.'

Mr Chaddha shook the proffered hand and said, 'I would be interested to know from what country you are from.'

Prem was through the door and out in the street in no time. He knew it was not polite of him to run away like that, but it was the only way that occurred to him. It was some time before he heard Hans running behind him. 'Wait!' Hans was shouting, but Prem neither waited nor looked back.

'Why did you go away?' Hans asked, when he had caught up; he sounded not aggrieved, merely surprised. 'I wanted to meet the Principal of your college for a discussion. There are many things in the educational policy in India I would like to have explained to me.' He tucked his arm into Prem's. 'Come, we will take the bus to my house and have conversation.'

Although he would have preferred to go home to Indu, Prem did not feel – especially after the effort of his precipitate flight from the college – that he had the strength to resist Hans. So soon they were with Kitty, who sat darning a big grey stocking. 'Well,' she said to Prem, 'quite the little stranger, aren't we?'

'You make him shy,' Hans accused her. He dusted a chair with his hand, then patted it and told Prem, 'Come, sit. I will tell you a news.'

'What news?' Kitty said. Hans winked at her heavily, but to no effect. 'That you're going away, you mean?'

'Ach!' Hans cried, 'now you have spoilt it!' Prem failed to get the point of this exchange, for he was looking up at the walls which, with the rains, had come out in patches of mildrew. He was surprised when Hans came and sat on the floor at his feet and placed a tender hand on his knee: 'Our friendship has meant much to me,' Hans said in a voice thick with feeling.

'How about a nice cup of tea?' Kitty said.

Hans became quite angry with her: 'We are talking here together, perhaps for the last time in the whole of our life . . .' He looked up at Prem, and his pale blue eyes behind the rimless spectacles were loving and sad. 'Who knows,' he sighed, 'when we can meet again?'

'Oh,' Prem said in surprise, 'you are going away?'

'What a song and dance about nothing,' Kitty said.

Hans frowned at her: 'You have no feeling for friendship.'

'I believe very much in friendship,' Prem said ardently. 'For me a friend is like a brother, only with a friend you can talk more than you can talk with your brother, and you tell him everything.' He met Kitty's stare, felt confused at having said so much and dropped his eyes like a shy young girl.

'The way you talk,' Kitty said calmly, 'Anybody'd think there wasn't any such thing as the Infinite.'

Hans became thoughtful. He say on the floor, with his legs drawn up and his chin resting gloomily on his knees. 'You are right,' he said after a while. 'I forget the source of my being and so become I attached to friends and other things which are only Maya.'

Kitty pushed the needle in and out of her grey stocking, darning with thick clumsy fingers. She said, 'We mustn't forget the Eternal Essence, must we?'

Prem felt sorry that Hans was going away and he wanted to say so. Only he felt shy, with Kitty sitting there so square and practical, darning her stocking. He did not wish his finer feelings to be disapproved of.

Hans got up. He said to Prem in a brisk manly way: 'Yes, now I am taking again the rucksack on the back. I am going to the south. There I hope perhaps to meet with a guru who will guide me.'

Prem swallowed and said, 'It is a pity our friendship cannot continue.' But he had wanted to say something much warmer, something expressive of all his deep feelings about friendship.

Hans shrugged and clapped his hands against his thighs in a gesture of resignation. 'We must be non-attached,' he said. 'If there is friend or enemy, if there it is hot or cold, our feeling must always be the same.' He trailed off rather and made the same resigned gesture as before. Prem said, 'I will think of you often.'

'People are always together in the One, aren't they?' Kitty said. She tried to bite her thread off with her teeth, couldn't and grumbled, 'Can't think who keeps running off with the scissors.'

'So,' Hans said, holding out his hand to Prem. Prem got up and took it and felt sad. Hans tried to smile; but looking up, Prem was surprised to notice that his eyes were swimming with tears. Prem was touched, but at the same time slightly guilty because he himself was not deeply enough stirred to bring up tears. He blinked his eyes several times but it was no use: he did not feel sad enough to want to cry. Maybe he no longer needed a friend as urgently as he had done. After all, he had Indu now.

She lay curled up on their big double bed, with her chin cupped in her hand and a thoughtful expression on her face. She asked, 'Do you think your friend would like kheer or carrot halwa?'

'Shall I telephone to his office and ask him?'

'For you perhaps it is a joke, but I have to make all preparations.'

He stretched himself out beside her and lay with his head close to hers and his chin, like hers, cupped in his hand.

'Inviting guests brings a lot of trouble to the woman of the house,' she said with an important frown.

Prem also looked solemn. 'I think it will be better to tell them not to come.'

She shot him a quick anxious glance. 'In your condition,' he said, still solemn, 'you must have all rest.'

But seeing the disappointed look on her face, he burst out laughing and darted his head forward quickly to rub his nose against hers.

'Thank you,' Indu said indignantly, 'today you are in a good mood for jokes.' She dusted at her nose and wrinkled it in an unconvincing display of distaste.

But she really was very serious about providing proper entertainment for their guests. On Sunday morning, when Prem woke up, she was already bustling about in the kitchen and shouting at the servant-boy. 'You owl! How many times must I tell you for korma the meat must be soaked in curds!' She shouted at Prem too when he showed himself in the kitchen: 'There is no need for you to come in here! Today we are all too busy to listen to any jokes from you!'

136

Prem hovered uncomfortably between the sitting-room and the bedroom. Soon the flat was full of delicious smells, of onions frying in clarified butter, of freshly ground spices and tender browned meat. Prem glimped into the kitchen and saw Indu deftly rolling mince balls between her palms, biting her lip in an effort of concentration, her bangles jingling and jangling up and down. Prem too began to be rather nervous. He wanted Raj and his wife to carry away a good impression of his household, so that on the way home they should say to one another, 'Prem's wife knows how to run her house'; and then Raj would no longer think of him as the inexperienced Ankhpur schoolboy that he had been, but as a settled husband and householder, on a par with Raj himself.

When everything was finished, Indu dressed herself in a pink georgette sari and gold ear-rings and was ready to receive their guests. Prem too was ready and both of them sat and waited. 'You are sure they will come?' Indu said, folding and unfolding her fingers. 'Of course – he promised,' Prem answered anxiously. Indu got up and bustled about in the kitchen for a while. When she came back, she said, 'Perhaps they could not find our house.' 'Oh, yes, it is very difficult to find,' Prem said, attempting a jocular tone which however he was too nervous to carry off. Indu did not even hear him: 'Oh,' she moaned, twisting her hands, 'what will happen to all the food I have prepared if they don't come?'

But soon afterwards steps were heard on the stairs. Raj came up, carrying Babli in his arms. While still on the stairs, he said in an accusing tone, 'You did not tell me your house was such a long way from the bus-stop.' His wife came behind him, square and smiling, wearing a green sari, printed all over with red and yellow roses, which sagged around her stout figure.

Raj put Babli down. 'She was tired and I had to carry her. She is quite heavy.' He wiped his forehead with a handkerchief. 'Look how I am sweating.'

Indu pinched Babli's cheek: 'What is your name?' Babli began to cry. 'She is shy with people she does not know,' Raj explained. 'Be quiet, or you will get a slap!'

Indu picked her up and thrust a sweetmeat into her mouth. 'Such a good girl I have never seen,' she said. Raj's wife smiled and smiled. Babli chewed the sweetmeat, a fat tear still quivering on her cheek.

Raj looked round the room. 'How much rent do you pay?' When

137

Prem told him, he shook his head: 'It is too much.' 'What to do?' Prem said. 'Nowadays rents are very high.' And he sighed the sigh of a family-man with many worries on his head.

Raj's wife was sitting with her legs wide apart and her hands folded in her lap. The green sari hung limply on her shoulder; it was also trailing on the floor around her feet, but she did not notice. She sat and smiled and looked at Indu's stomach.

Raj tapped the wall. 'You can see it is a very cheap construction.' Prem also tapped: 'When it rains, the water comes in,' he said. Raj shook his head and wisely pursed his lips: 'The landlord should not be allowed to charge so much rent.'

Indu was holding Babli's wrist and making her clap her hands: 'My granny's gone to market,' she sang to her.

'Landlords must be checked from profiteering,' Raj said severely. Prem nodded and also looked severe.

'For four bowls she did pay, but one got broken on the way,' Indu sang, clapping Babli's hands in time to the tune. Raj's wife said suddenly, 'What month?' Indu blushed and smiled and turned aside her head. But soon they were deep in whispered conversation.

'You must stand up for your rights as a tenant,' Raj said. 'You have your family to think of.'

'Especially in the nights,' Indu was whispering to Raj's wife.

Babli plucked at Indu's sari and shouted, 'Sing more!'

'And soon there will be one more, I think,' Raj said almost coyly. Prem looked down at his feet and smiled. 'You will have to think how to cut down your expenses.'

'It will be a boy,' Raj's wife said.

Indu caught Babli's hands again and sang, 'Oh, how angry granny got!'

'I can see from the way you are carrying,' Raj's wife said.

'She stamped her foot and home she trot!'

'You will be surprised when you find how much even one baby costs,' Raj said.

The servant-boy came and spread a mat on the floor. He was wearing a new shirt and looked proud and dignified. Indu followed him into the kitchen and soon they both returned with brass trays on which stood little bowls filled with food. They all sat down on the mat and the servant-boy watched them with an air of importance.

'Ah,' said Raj. Steam and delicious smells came floating out of the little bowls. Indu looked anxious as her guests began to eat.

138

'Very nice,' Raj's wife pronounced after her first few mouthfuls, swaying her head from side to side in appreciation.

Indu glowed, but she murmured, 'It is only our plain home food.'

Raj had his mouth full of rice. He said, 'It seems your wife is a very good cook.' Then Prem felt really proud.

Esmond in India
Ruth Prawar Jhabvala

A master of both the comic and the serious, Ruth Prawar Jhabvala's richly ripe Indian comedy of manners strips bare a certain section of affluent Indian society particularly vulnerable to the seductions of an imperial presence. In the contrast she draws between two very different families and their daily lives – their squabbles, their politics, their love affairs, their expectations – she brilliantly and wittily crystallizes some of the confusions that bedevilled India at the dawn of Independence.

'A writer of genius – a master story-teller' – *Sunday Times*

A Passage to India
E. M. Forster

'That Marabar Case' threw the city of Chandrapore into a fever of racial feeling. Miss Quested on a visit from England to the man she expected to marry, showed an interest in Indian ways of life which was frowned on by the sun-baked British community. And their prejudice appeared to be justified when she returned, alone and distressed, from an excursion to the caves with a young Indian doctor. But what had really happened?

The Siege of Krishnapur
J. G. Farrell

In the Spring of 1857, life for the British at Krishnapur, conscious of the benefits civilization has brought to India, confident of the March of Progress embodied in the Great Exhibition, is orderly and genteel. Only Mr Hopkins, the Collector, senses danger.

Then the mutiny, violent and bloody, comes to Krishnapur; the British community retreats into the Residency to fight for its life; and for the first time European civilization confronts the world it thinks it rules.

Raj

Charles Allen

Here is a nostalgic and affectionate portrait, in both words and pictures, of life in the great years of the British Raj; of the world of *dak* bungalows, Cold Weather Tours, Governor's Camps, Orders of Precedence, fancy-dress balls and calling cards; of Walers, hogspears, trophies, Roorkee chairs, bedding rolls and soda-water machines. It offers a fresh and wholly original approach to the Anglo-Indian experience and an invaluable historical record of a vanished age.

The Great Mutiny

India 1857

Christopher Hibbert

'By far the best single-volume description of the mutiny yet written' – *Economist*

'A good book can always be expected from Christopher Hibbert, but this time he has excelled himself' – *Sunday Telegraph*

'A first-rate book, well researched, beautifully written, and so exciting that I had difficulty in laying it down' – Philip Magnus in the *Sunday Times*

An Area of Darkness

V. S. Naipaul

Coming from a family which left India only two generations ago, V. S. Naipaul felt that his roots lay in India. But the country and its attitudes remained outside his experience, in an 'area of darkness', until, with some apprehension, he spent a year there. He arrived at Bombay, then travelled as far north as Kashmir, east to Calcutta and south to Madras. Here he shares his experience of India generously and gives the reader deep insight into a country and a writer's mind.

'Tender, lyrical, explosive . . . excellent' – John Wain

'Most compelling and vivid' – V. S. Pritchett

James Morris

The *Pax Britannica* trilogy

This brilliantly and superbly written triptych depicts the rise and decline of the British Empire. The three volumes – 'a vast panorama of history, glorious, savage, sad and painful' – combine in an impressionistic evocation of a great historical movement. Graced by the hand of a chronicler and interpreter whose eye for detail and ear for anecdote are combined with a formidable scholarship, the *Pax Britannica* trilogy encapsulates for the reader all the poetry and panache of that glittering adventure.

Heaven's Command: An Imperial Progress

Describing the rise of the Empire until its apogee in 1897, this first volume was praised by *The Times* as '*a tour de force*, majestically sure of touch, rich in tone, comprehensive in range'.

Pax Britannica: The Climax of an Empire

The second volume elaborates on the sprawling and magnificent edifice of Empire at its moment of climax at the Diamond Jubilee in 1897. It is, as Dennis Potter wrote, 'at once a celebration and an elegy, a triumphant catalogue and a funeral oration, a tribute and an apology'.

Farewell The Trumpets: An Imperial Retreat

The imperial retreat from glory, finishing with the death of Sir Winston Churchill in 1965, is charted in this last volume, described by the *Scotsman* as 'totally captivating. Throughout [James Morris] succeeds, as Kipling did, in capturing the flavour of Empire, its triumphs and glories, and above all its people.'

Barbara Pym

Excellent Women

Mildred was quite capable of dealing with the stock situations of life.

In fact her handling of births, marriages, deaths, jumble sales and garden fêtes ruined by the weather was masterly. It is the introduction of new and exotic neighbours that pulls her up short.

Barbara Pym is a rare and subtle writer. Unerring, acerbic, penetrating, she unrolls with deceptive gentleness a world that is still part of the English social scene.

'Her sense of brilliant comedy is a direct inheritance from Jane Austen' – *Hibernia*

'I could go on reading her for ever' – A. L. Rowse in *Punch*

A Glass of Blessings

'The subtlest of her books – the sparkle on first acquaintance has been succeeded by the deeper brilliance of established art' – Philip Larkin

Wilmet Forsyth is fairly young, good looking, well dressed, well looked after, suitably husbanded and rather bored. Her interest wanders to the nearby Anglo-Catholic church and its three unmarried priests and on to Piers Longridge whose enigmatic overtures are rather intriguing.

The story of an innocent at large is, as usual, handled brilliantly and tactfully by a writer whose sense of social comedy, and whose penetration, are of the highest order.

'I could go on reading her for ever' – A. L. Rowse in *Punch*